Guerrilla
of the
Niger Delta

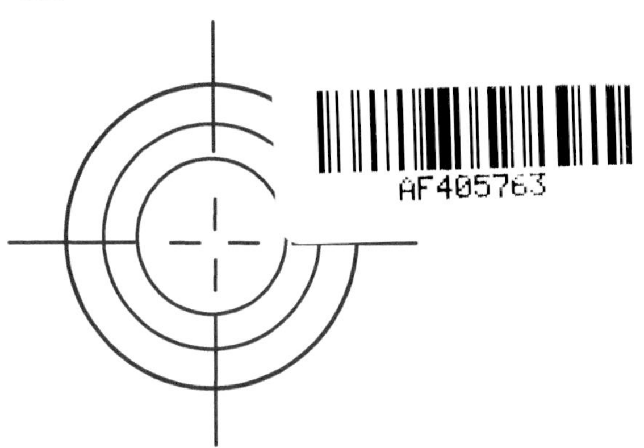

Guerrilla
of the
Niger Delta

Don Veta

ISBN: 978-978-58069-3-9

This is a work of fiction. All characters and events are the product of the author's imagination. Any resemblance to any person, living or dead, is coincidental.

Published in Nigeria by Winepress Publishing
An imprint of Noirledge Limited

Noirledge Limited
Suite 223, Ogun-Osun River Basin Development Authority,
Adjacent Palms Shopping Mall, Ring-Road, Ibadan
Tel: +234 809 816 4359 | +234 805 316 4359
Email: winepress@noirledge.com | www.noirledge.com
twitter.com/noirledge | facebook.com/noirledge | instagram.com/noirledge

Winepress titles are available for bulk purchase for educational and corporate use. Special editions, personalised covers and excerpts from our titles can also be made available at special rates. For more information, contact our Sales Department via winepress@noirledge.com or +234 809 8164 359.

Cover Design: Don Veta/Noirledge Studios
Book Design: Servio Gbadamosi/Noirledge Studios

Dedication

To God Almighty, for His love and care. To my late father, Aaron Obukohwo Uviemarierie, for nurturing me through the stormy waters. To Patrick Poirson and Patricia Pope, as you sojourn on, know that humanity will always miss you. A warm thought of affectionate love for you my little Angel…with you comes fond memories, and the drive to keep pushing boundaries.
Lastly, to all elements of change, dead or alive, know that your struggle is never in vain.

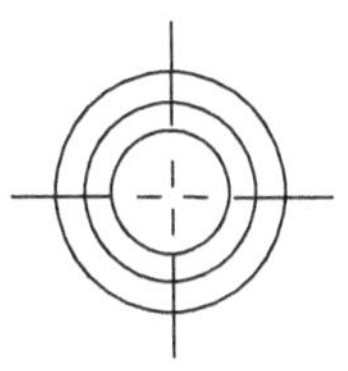

Prelude

The Economic Community of West African States Monitoring Group (ECOMOG) was disbanded because of secret, multilateral, armed missions. Some of the soldiers took part in secret missions, largely appropriating resources for their personal gain. These were stripped of all their military benefits and were dishonourably discharged for actions unbecoming of military officers. Many ex-soldiers, needing to survive, became angry groups of mercenaries. Spreading across the length and breadth of the West African region, many organised their freedom-fighting skills into private guerrilla activities. Sergeant Kiddo is one of those soldiers. He served in Sierra Leone, on the Special Unit Squad.

With the rebellion in the creeks, the activities of militants and mercenaries caused the oil cartel to lose hold on their business grip in the Niger-Delta. These events soon came to a climax, and the government took action to bring them in for evading government prosecution and abusing government funds meant for the development of the region. The oil barons, in a bid to hold on to their rewarding business interests, enlisted the services of Sergeant Malaya Rogers (aka Kiddo). His mission was to help carry out an urgent, top-secret assignment that would help preserve the Brotherhood.

He woke up as the alarm on his watch lying on the end table went off. He reached for it and looked at the time—it was 4 a.m. Jumping into his pyjama trousers, he takes his laptop from the bedside table along with his modem and trudged into the living room, which was faintly illuminated with light from the kitchen. He sat on the couch, and switching on the laptop, he inserted the modem. While the computer booted, he walked to the refrigerator to get some juice, and after pouring it into a glass, Kiddo headed back to the living-room. After sipping slowly, he placed the glass of orange juice on the table made of blown glass. He clicked on the Mozilla icon on the laptop, and logged into his Facebook account. His message indicator showed that there was a message. He opened it immediately and clicked on the attached picture. The photo of a man dressed in a black suit appeared. The man was a U.S. diplomat authorised to liquidate some of the oil facilities built by the Development Commission with proceeds accrued from oil subsidies. Kiddo dashed into his bedroom with one swift motion and returned with a smartphone.

Switching on the Wi-Fi and connecting it to the laptop, he downloaded the picture into the phone. Then he put on a black leather jacket and blue jeans, picked up the laptop and shoved it into a backpack, while hurriedly downing the remaining contents of his glass.

Never mind; it's already 5 a.m., he thought to himself as he swiftly opened the door and left the house. In his small garage was parked a black Harley-Davidson power bike, delivered to him the previous week for a mission he undertook across Seme border; a commercial border town, between the countries of Nigeria and the Republic of Bénin through which stolen and used cars were smuggled. A chief customs officer had been making life unbearable for a smuggling syndicate and their operations. The black Harley-Davidson was a show of appreciation from the syndicate for the effortless way Kiddo had removed the pain in their necks.

Climbing onto the machine, he revved it until his heart pumped and adrenaline ran through his veins, mixed with raw excitement reverberating through his entire being. He raced through Governor's Avenue with the wind in his ears at 250 kilometres per hour, enjoying the acceleration of the epic piece of metal between his knees. On his launch, not even the cool breeze of the early morning, whipping against his face, could deter his hands and feet from the pedals on the bike. He revved harder all through the highway at 160 miles per hour leading off the avenue, lifting dried leaves and resurrecting dust along a dead path. The cold wind acted as a coolant on his mind and body, making the ride enjoyable. He negotiated the power bike off the avenue, and onto a narrow path, leading to the river bank at the end of an obscure road.

Riding for over another half hour on the dusty path, he caught sight of a farmhouse. On reaching there, he brought the metal piece to a halt, and walked over to the farmhouse. The quiet morning atmosphere was slightly intimidating as he looked around to make sure that there were no surprises in store for him. This was one thing he never allowed to happen to him. He had come to know that in this mercenary business, no one was to be trusted, especially the piper who played the tune.

Satisfied that the place was safe, he whipped out his smartphone and scrolled to the most recent message. He reads the instructions sent to him, and then walked to the front door. Lifting a jasmine flower pot set nearby, he retrieved a single key with which he opened the door leading to the farmhouse. The interior did not betray anything short of what Kiddo would have expected from a farmhouse ordinarily used for this kind of delivery. All furniture and fixtures were in their right places. A huge Mona Lisa portrait gracefully adorned one end of the room. He walked over to the table where a neatly-bounded box of fine oakwood had been placed. He brought out his stiletto knife and eased off the bounding strips used to encase the box and opened it. He saw the brand-new pieces of a dismantled assault rifle. As he moved to bring out the pieces one after the other, his cell phone rang, startling him.

"Agrrh." he groaned, beads of sweat dotting his forehead. He wiped the sweat off with the back of his right hand and placed the phone against his ear with his left hand. A thick baritone voice hit his earlobe saying, "Underneath the box is fifty percent of the agreed fee". Kiddo immediately turned the box over, and he saw a small package with a tiny padlock on it. He ripped it off with a twist of his stiletto knife, dipped his right hand into a bag, and grabbed a bundle of hundred-dollar bills, admiring the crisp notes in the dim light of the farmhouse. A slow smile played around his lips. As if the man on the other end of the line was monitoring his every move, he heard his voice continue, "The other fifty you will get on delivery. Remember we expect nothing short of perfect on this one". The line went dead. Kiddo tucked away the stack of hundred-dollar bills and started to assemble the assault rifle.

The Mission

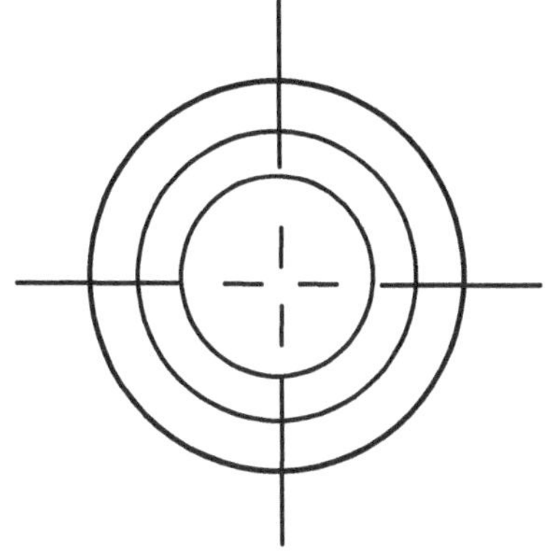

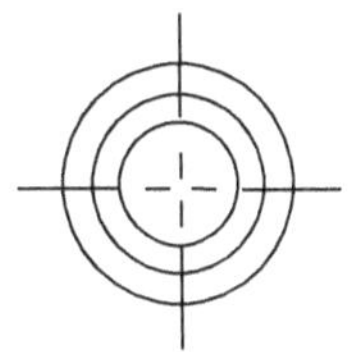

Ambushed

The intense, tropical African, morning sun expelled its venom on the grass at the opposite side of the bush path leading to a hut which spread over almost two and a half acres of land. A close look at the path revealed that the route had not been used by passers-by in a while. The state of the hut showed years of abandonment.

The mud which had been used to build it had deteriorated into tiny grains of sand, which had fallen off in patches, revealing the bamboo and bamboo strings used in constructing the frames that held the hut together. The windows were now a feasting ground for termites, geckos and lizards, animals that overwhelmed the old windows and doors. A simple look at the hut quickly dismissed any thought of inhabitants living in such a place. Yet a distorted sound scratched through the door, and heavy breathing made itself perceptible amidst the sounds coming from a television set.

The interior of the hut showed three sets of old worn-out chairs, each small piece competing for space within the trifling room. The voice from the television set became audible amidst the breathing and panting which came from the adjacent door facing the tiny living room.

"This is the news at eight," a female broadcaster's voice announced. Como, dressed in boxers, was in a corner of the hut adorned with the best of the latest electronic gadgets and devices. The air was stale and reeked with terrible odours from pieces of clothing thrown carelessly on the floor. The surroundings had not been cleaned for a long while. The news went on. Como was at the other end of the room intensely engrossed in his routine morning exercises, sweating profusely and breathing heavily. He stood up from the floor after doing 50 intense push ups. One look at his muscular six-foot-tall, dark-skinned 225-pound frame is enough to make any professional boxer, wrestler or mixed martial artist think twice. Como dashed across the room of the small hut disappearing through a tiny passage.

Simultaneously, in the deep interiors of the creeks were a group of men numbering ten. All dressed in red bibs, with black-rimmed edges on the neck and the waistline, worn over black, tight-fitting jeans and army style boots, as they sat on bamboo chairs in the incomprehensible forest region. They chanted war tunes in low tones, each of them inspecting their AK 47—a contribution to the art of war by the Soviet Union, the AK assault rifle, the Automatic Killer. The AK is an excellent weapon of choice for maximum penetration when shooting through heavy foliage, walls, a vehicle's metal body, tissue and bone. The AK-47 cartridge produces significant wounding as the bullet tumbles through the air at 715 miles a second.

Smoking marijuana cigarettes, they loaded their sidearm; the Italian Beretta 92FS, a 9-millimetre military killing machine. The German-manufactured Parabellum ballistic round for this semiautomatic Beretta 92FS provides exceptional deadly accuracy. Como stood straight, as if looking at an imaginary mirror as he held a Beretta CX4 Storm, a lightweight self-loading pistol and a calibre carbine machine gun hang over his left shoulder. Dressed up in black tactical gear, he looked around. His tiny eyes rolled in their sockets as if searching for something. They fell on a pair of black boots. He reached for them and picked them up, and started to loosen the laces. The loud forceful encroachment of the militants could be heard under the wispy sounds of the leaves in the lush green vegetation of the forest. Fully-fitted in military style uniforms, like guerrillas they violently tore through the bush in a single file, leaving only the audible noise of leaves rustling in their wake. Como, now fully dressed, took a quick look at himself. He could have been mistaken for a senior military officer with a mission! His mission, a stark contrast to the Middle East style of warfare. He turned around and cast a quick glance at his weapons, just to assure himself he had not forgotten any of them. As he was turning to leave the room, his eyes fell on the photograph of the American ambassador who was on the news, shaking hands with his Nigerian counterpart. Como walked a little closer to the television and increased the volume.

"The US ambassador who arrived in the country last night will, along with the Minister of Petroleum, tour some of the facilities that the Federal government has initiated in partnership with the US government, an initiative to help reduce the flaring of gas within the Niger-Delta regions of the south-south." Como, who had been listening impatiently, rose to his feet in anger and smashed the television set, which crumbled into pieces at his feet. Snorting in rage at the news he just heard, he turned abruptly and walked out of the room.

The sun danced gracefully and reflected its golden light on the surface of the river. Birds chirped in the nearby trees, which adorned the beautiful landscape of the riverside, where the PT-90 riverine combat boat, codenamed "Crocodile" lay in wait. The Crocodile is an extremely fast, amphibious, military assault craft used to transport soldiers and supplies—a treasure to mercenaries for their speed and agile manoeuvring when navigating in the coastal areas in the creeks. The PT-90 is essential to the efficiency of their coastal activities. Sounds and rumblings came through the dense forest. Along the narrow path towards the river, the men all filed out from the bushes in a horizontal line beside the PT-90. The man standing in the middle issued out an order, "take the Crocodile into the water!"

Immediately, four of the men emerged from the line. They jumped at the Crocodile and started pulling it into the water, while the others ran alongside them towards the boat. They got the Crocodile off the shore and climbed into it. The boat immediately roared into full motion and glided away, disappearing into the heart of the creeks.

The early morning sun rose on the serene environment that engulfed the corporate headquarters of the multinational petroleum exploration building. The centre of endless boisterous activities, recent militant interference had compromised government projects for the development of the Niger-Delta region. It was the first day of the busy week ahead. It marked the arrival of the U.S. ambassador, who had been invited to liquidate some projects co-sponsored by the U.S. and Nigerian governments that were just compromised. Different brands of luxury cars were parked outside the entrance to the building. The buildings spread over several acres of land. At a glance it resembled the skyline of buildings in Dubai. It was rumoured that one walk inside those magnificent buildings is what inspired the life of embezzlement characterised by high-profile Nigerian oil firms, officials, and oil barons.

The twin doors swung open, and the Minister of Petroleum Resources of the Republic, in step with the U.S. ambassador in company with top oil bureaucrats and security agents, streamed out of the building. Security officers immediately posted guards at various entrances leading to the parking lot. As the U.S. Ambassador exchanged pleasantries with those who had come out to bid him farewell, the security officers ushered them into the waiting cars and made sure they were well secured. Agent Andre, the chief intelligence officer attached to the U.S. Ambassador's entourage, put a call through to police headquarters, affirming that the inspection team was about to leave for the project sites.

"All protocol complete. We are heading towards the bridge, en route the commissioning site at Ogbotobor," Agent Andre informed headquarters waiting for a reply.

"Information confirmed," the voice from the other end of the line replied. "Safe trip, and keep us informed of future developments.

"Yes sir, over and out," replied Agent Andre.

He switched off the radio and beckoned to two officers who stood by their car, waiting for instructions. After they had received the command, they reacted immediately. Como walked through the tall thick grass. His cell phone rang. He dipped his hand into his coat, brought out his Nokia navigator phone from his pocket, and answered the call in a deep voice with an Ijaw accent. The Ijaw languages are traditionally a distinct branch of the Eastern and Western Ijo—of the Niger-Congo family. The traditional languages of the Izon people of Southern Nigeria.

"Hello, sir, target left ten minutes ago. Confirm location, I will be with you soon."

A voice thundered from the mouthpiece of the phone onto his ear.

"Ok, sir." He switched off the phone and walked on.

The Crocodile with its fierce-looking occupants roared on the high sea with its tidal waves. The cell phone of the leader of the gang rang loudly. He quickly reached for it in his pocket, and strained to listen. The sounds from the roaring Crocodile and the wind from the sea made it difficult for him to hear. The voice came out faintly.

"Target is within twenty minutes; all units on ground; copy that."

"Copied," he replied. He immediately issued an order in his Ijaw dialect.

"Merchandise is close, coming through route X, off the baseline by the market axis," he shouted out to the man behind the wheel. There was a sudden increase in the roaring of the Crocodile, and immediately it sailed with the men into the tide of the river. The entourage drove along Minister Lane in the isolated forest of Palm Groove Avenue which housed thousands of palm trees sandwiching both paths of the road. Dry leaves falling from the trees littered the drive way. In the far distance, a rickety Volkswagen car came along, smoking heavily. The car jerked and coughed on the road. The driver, an unkept, old-looking man with a big, round belly, the size, which made it difficult for him to button his scruffy looking black shirt, worn over a dirty white t-shirt, was trying to keep the car on course.

Suddenly the engine gave way to serious overheating and he was forced to bring the car to a halt. The fragile, old-looking man opened the door and came out.

Coughing profusely, he wiped the exhaust pipe smoke polluting the atmosphere from his face, staggered to the rear of the car, trying desperately to get to the engine. Nevertheless, he struggled with the latch, his youthful vigour reduced, his frail frame a testament to his age. The U.S. Ambassador's car came along the same path. The aide attached to the first car saw the Volkswagen stuck in the middle of the road and asked the chauffeur to stop. The car glided to a halt, forcing the other vehicles behind to stop.

"CSO, what is the matter?" the minister asked his chief security officer grimacing in a well-polished voice.

"I will find out at once, sir." The chief security officer immediately radioed his colleague.

"Alpha, alpha, why are we stopping? Copy."

"Alpha, alpha, there's a broken-down vehicle on the road, sir! Copy," the aide in the first car, Corporal James, replied.

"A broken-down vehicle, sir." he informed the minister. "How long will this take?" he asked, looking at his watch. Meanwhile, the U.S. ambassador sat calmly, looking at both of them.

"We have a schedule to respect," he added.

"I know, sir, let me see."

Immediately, he opened his door, came out of the car and walked towards other "officers" assigned to the team. The other security officers saw him from the side mirror of their cars. They all came down swiftly and walked towards the car. The old man grappling with the car lifted his eyebrows when he saw them coming over to him. He reached for his cell phone and dialled a number. The old man became agitated as they closed in on him. Hands shaking, he responded in a grumbled voice.

Corporal James who was already in front of him, seeing him struggling to return the phone to his pocket, called out to him, "Sir?"

The phone dropped from his hand and fell to the ground, spilling its contents on the tarred road.

"Oh, my!" he cried, "My phone!" He bent down and tried to pick up the scattered pieces. Ignoring them, Corporal James had almost reached the old man when the security officer's voice thundered through, "Confirm position!"

"Position positive!" Corporal James immediately ended the call. Hot sweat poured down his face.

Corporal James was the first officer to reach the old man. The rest of the officers were left with the chief security officer standing and watching the scenario from the car as they mounted guard over the convoy with care.

"Will you get this car off the road?" Corporal James ordered the man.

"It can't move," cried the old man, as he struggled to pick up the pieces of what was left of his cell phone.

"What is the situation?" the chief security officer's voice filtered through Corporal James's hearing device on his ear.

"Completely broken-down vehicle, sir," replied Corporal James.

"Mobilise and remove for quick extraction, copy?" replied the CSO.

"Copy, sir," Corporal James replied.

Switching off his device, he turned round and issued orders to the rest of the security officers.

"Guys, let's go!" Immediately the six of them pounced on the Volkswagen Beetle car and began pushing it off the road.

Scanning surreptitiously the nearby grasses and trees, the chief security officer suddenly noticed some suspicious movement within the nearby bushes.

"It's a set up!" he yelled, but before he could complete the sentence, gunshots poured out from the surrounding foliage. Three of the security officers were hit. In a swift move, the old man took a dive into his car which was already bullet-ridden. Corporal James and the other two security officers also took cover behind the Volkswagen which now served as a shield from the bullets, and they aimed in the direction of the gunshots. The screeching sound of a Harley-Davidson roaring into motion with Kiddo waving a FN-P90 assault rifle in his left hand skidded into view on the motorcycle. Jumping off the Harley -Davidson Kiddo cut down everything within his path with a Fabrique Nationale FN-P90 submachine gun—a Belgian-made killing device using high velocity subsonic ammunition. Como and his men camouflaging within the thick dense foliage were forced to retreat, due to the unexpected superior firepower of the intruder.

Inspector Davis rode his 2000-model BMW along the busy roundabout in the heart of the oil city. When he drove through the third-junction roundabout, his cell phone rang from the interior of the dashboard where he usually kept it. He hated struggling to reach for the phone whenever driving, especially when out on an official assignment like this one. He reached for the phone and snapped it up. Inspector Davis answered before he determined who the caller was. The deep voice of the Commissioner of Police came on the line.

"All units, this is an emergency! The Minister of Petroleum Resources and his U.S. counterpart are being ambushed along Minister Lane. I repeat the Minister of Petroleum and his U.S. visitor have been ambushed along Minister Lane."

Davis, as if possessed by a thousand demons, snapped the phone shut and threw it on the passenger's seat. He pressed his feet on the gas pedal of the BMW, and immediately swung into action.

The bodies of the dead agents were strewn on the road where the assault had just taken place. Kiddo walked triumphantly like one who had just won the lottery, pointing his FN-P90 towards the bodies lying on the ground. He inspected them one after the other, making sure that they were all dead.

Kiddo then walked towards the black SUV where the minister and the U.S. Ambassador were still seated. They were visibly shaking with fright, terror written all over them. On reaching the car, he swung the door open, pointing the submachine gun at both men, who wilfully surrendered to him. Pleading for their lives, they begged in voices doused in anguish.

"Please, don't hurt us!" With a wave of the gun, he ordered both men out. They scrambled for the door, as the reality of death dawned on them, wondering who would be the first one to go. In their confused state, they fell over each other, and hit the tarred road simultaneously. Kiddo took hold of the ambassador in one hand and raised him up. He ordered the minister with a wave of the gun to stand up, the gun nozzle pointing at him.

"Please, don't kill me!" the minister cried out. "Tell me what you want, and I will make sure you get it. Please, spare my life, I have a family."

Kiddo heard the sound of an approaching car. He turned in the direction of the oncoming vehicle, and made a quick calculation of its distance. He reckoned the car was closer than he thought. Kiddo quickly calculated his exit route and dragged the U.S. Ambassador along and disappeared into the thick bush, leaving the minister behind. Screeching to a halt, Inspector Davis almost hit the transfixed minister who had been left kneeling at the centre of the road. He saw the figures of two men disappear into the thick undergrowth. He rushed out of the BMW and yelled.

"Where did they go?" Davis asked the still shaken and terrified minister who was unable to answer. Davis wondered for a moment which path to take. By intuition rather than out of experience, he followed a path, which, he later confirmed, was the right one the kidnapper and his victim had taken. Running along that path, he put a call through to the Divisional Headquarters for backup.

"Alpha, Alpha, the U.S. Ambassador was not found at the scene. A possible kidnapping has taken place, requesting back-up. The suspected kidnapper is presumed to be heading towards the bridge head at Ujenu. Back-up needed. Repeat. The suspect is heading towards the Ujenu head bridge, over and out."

Then he heard the sound of a PT-90 roaring away from the bridge head. He stopped running and took a deep breath slowing down his steps. Walking out of the bush, he saw the Passport 90 in the distance, at vanishing point heading for the high sea. Davis almost keeled over. Exhausted and trying to catch his breath, he rested for a while, after which he made his way back to the crime scene. Examining the extent of the attack, he discovered a full squad of the Joint Task Force dead. The Joint Task Force was a team comprising Armed Forces personnel from all the various service forces, a constabulary force the government had set up to help curb illegal oil bunkering (smugglers) and kidnapping within the region. Inspector Davis put a call through and paramedics appeared to help evacuate the dead bodies.

The head of the Task Force, Captain Danbata, saw Davis walk out of the bush and head toward him wearily. Captain Danbata approached Inspector Davis, and they consulted in a low tone. Davis explained to him what he found when he arrived, the events and pointed out the possible escape route that the kidnapper used. As the paramedics left with the remains of the dead officers, other personnel searched and thoroughly examined the area, looking for evidence in their investigation. Spent bullet shells were also retrieved. They made notes and took photographs of the entire crime scene. After sealing off the crime scene, they departed.

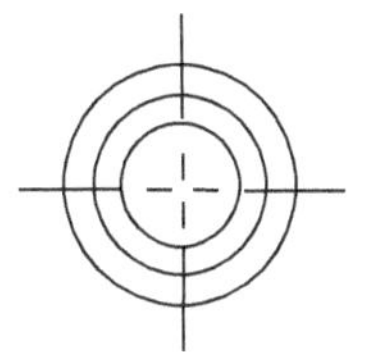

The Mission

It was seven in the morning. The sharp shrill of the bedside alarm clock pierced through Delano's nerves interrupting his long and arduous dream. The rays of the sun streamed through the sky-blue curtains, flooding the bedroom with the morning light. Delano struggled to open his eyes, squinting against the bright light; he stretched lazily and rolled over to look at the bedside clock. Groaning, he pulled off the bed covers and swiftly got up. His masculine body was well built with broad shoulders, and standing veins covered in hair ran through his arms. He was as hairy as a fox! Wearing a pair of boxers only, a striped, red Tommy Hilfiger kind, he went into the kitchen for his morning coffee. Putting on the kettle, he waited for several seconds and his instant coffee was ready just the way he liked it. He went back into the living room with a steaming mug in his hand and sipped slowly, the taste and aroma of the coffee awakening his brain and taste buds. After a short while, he turned on the television set, and went to the door which led to the entrance into his apartment, and opened it to reveal a well-cut lawn and neatly trimmed flowers.

Delano cautiously looked to the right and left of the crescent, which looked deserted. Picking up the newspaper lying at the door post, he went back inside and plunged himself into the couch in the living room, and opened the daily news section. The caption, "U.S. Ambassador kidnapped in Nigeria", caught his eye. Immediately, he flipped over to the page. He barely started to read the story, when a news flash came on the television screen. Jerry Sawyer, news anchor with the CBS news network, thundered out:

"The Secretary of State, briefing a reporter from the White House this morning, said there is an indication that the kidnapped

U.S. Ambassador who was abducted in the Niger-Delta in South-South, Nigeria by alleged militants fighting the government of Nigeria, might still be alive."

Delano's eyes widened in surprise. He listened with captivated attention as the news anchor continued.

"The U.S. President has requested his Secretary of Defense to immediately make arrangements to send one of the country's finest Marine officers to Nigeria to assist in the rescue of the U.S. Ambassador."

Jerry Sawyer was still anchoring the news when Delano stood up from the couch and headed for the bathroom.

The New York Police Department (NYPD) was a beehive of activities; officers on duty always had work to do. While officers at the State Department were going about their normal routine at the Force, Delano drove his Porsche coupe onto the police department's premises. He parked at the front entrance of the State Department. Wearing tight-fitting, blue denim pants, a white police tee shirt, and well-polished black leather boots, Delano walked hurriedly into the station. His gaze fell on a note lying on his desk as soon as he entered into his office. Delano looked at it cautiously and called out to Barbara Randall, the lady officer sitting opposite his desk—a beautiful six-foot-tall, African American lady with all the right radiance and poise, an excellent officer. Delano admired her from the first moment he laid eyes on her. He tried to make her his as he professed his love. He once told her that until his last breath, he would attempt to win her heart. She was also attracted to Delano but she didn't want the hassle of the job. Once, Delano had asked her to marry him, but she had declined his offer. She couldn't live with the loss of his life and the loss of his love. She told him so.

"My kids will know their father, and he will always be there for them," Barbara once whispered. Eventually, Delano won and together they shared numerous passionate moments. After a while though, the situation between them had gone bad when Delano found out she had been cheating on him with another officer in the same precinct. This revelation had made Delano put a considerable distance between them. He avoided her by every means possible, and staying away had become an option. He definitely still had a burning desire for her. But today he called out to her,

"Hey, Barbara?" Barbara raised her head to look at him. He waved the sealed paper before her, as if to say, "What is this?"

Barbara pointed to the superintendent's office.

"Said you should see him whenever you got in."

"Trouble?" he asked.

"Bet you figured that one out yourself." With that she turned her attention back to the computer in front of her. Delano looked startled. He paused, and on an afterthought, he walked to the superintendent's office and knocked gently on the glass door. The superintendent raised his head and immediately waved him in. As Delano walked into the office, everyone turned their attention towards the office.

"Delano, we have a special assignment for you, and it requires you traveling to Africa." Delano tuned out the superintendent.

"Special assignment?" exclaimed Delano. "Wait a minute, superintendent, did you say Africa?"

The superintendent nodded his head with an expressionless face.

"No way, not this time," Delano declared.

"Yes, son?"

Delano gazed at him, because whenever he used the word "Son." then it was definitely something he couldn't avoid doing. He had worked with the man for years and knew when he was serious.

"Why Africa, sir?" he asked.

"It is all over the news," replied the superintendent.

"And what about it, sir?"

"The Presidency wants you to go to Nigeria and help rescue the U.S. Ambassador".

"But why me, sir?" he grumbled. "I have just returned from one hell."

"Son!" the superintendent exclaimed. Their gazes locked. The superintendent stood up from his chair and walked over to him. Patting him on the shoulder, he tried to explain why they felt he was the right man for the job. Everyone outside was watching them in the little glass office. As Delano turned and walked back to the door, everyone scrambled back to their desks. He headed straight to his desk and removed some of his personal effects from his drawers into a bag. He did the same with the lower drawers, bringing out some more of his personal effects, and loading them into a box he brought out from under his table. Satisfied that he needed no more of the stuff remaining in his work station, he walked out of the office. Barbara's eyes had a look of trepidation as she watched him take his leave. Delano was one of the finest Marines in the United States. The fact is, Delano just returned from a mission in Asia, where (ASEAN) the Association of Southeast Asian Nations, helped to quell a militant rebel threat to the region. Barbara felt much for him, and above all she knew deep down in her heart that this was the time he would have needed her most as he left for his assigned duties. She sighed still watching him head towards his car, enter and drive off.

The recent face lift given to the Murtala Mohammed International Airport in Nigeria, one of the country's foremost airports after independence, showed better infrastructural development within the aviation industry in the country.

Traveling and returning passengers were flocking at the various terminals, going about their various activities. The travellers were patiently awaiting the call for their flights, while those who had just arrived were sorting themselves out with the immigration officers. Delano walked straight to meet the checking agent who, on seeing him, regarded him with disdain, waving him to move to the left-hand side to join a group of others and nationals he asked to wait.

The checking agent swore under his breath in Nigerian Pidgin language, "Na so una dey do us for that side" —an attitude which was gradually becoming a norm at the airport. This was the strategy most of these officers now used to show their level of contempt towards foreigner people coming in from other countries. These airport agents also considered this new attitude as retaliation against the inhumane treatment, which many Nigerians who travelled abroad received from their foreign contemporaries.

Delano waited with other passengers faced with similar protocol problems. After waiting patiently for a while, he became uncomfortable, wondering why they were asked to wait after being cleared already. All that was left for the clearing agent to do was to check out their luggage. Davis walked into the hall and immediately recognised Delano from the photograph he was holding and, walked straight up to the security guard and excused the guard. They had a brief chat, and the guard looked over his shoulder at Delano. Their gazes locked, and the guard smiled at him. Delano feared trouble. Quickly he calculated his next move. No one gets used to trouble; you only face it headlong when it comes. That had always been his policy, and despite the fact that he had become used to situations like these as a result of his many missions, he never for once compromised his preventive measures. Davis walked to him and stretched out his hand.

"Mr. Delano, Davis, from the Central Investigating Bureau (CIB)."

Inspector Davis flashed his National Police Identification card. Delano took a quick scan at the details, looked at him, stretched his hand as well, and they shook hands.

"This way, sir." Davis pointed the way out. Davis took hold of his luggage; Delano hesitated for a while, but Davis smiled at him. As he reluctantly but gently gave him the luggage, they walked out through the passage. Davis walked ahead of him towards a Peugeot 406 with the inscription, "Nigeria Police Force", and opened the door of the rear seat and ushered Delano in.

The key worked. The hotel room door opened to a lavishly furnished suite. Davis walked in, followed by Delano. He placed the luggage on the three-piece settee.

"Make yourself comfortable. First thing tomorrow, you will meet the Commissioner of Police for counter terrorism and you will be further briefed on your mission."

"Ok, thanks, I appreciate your assistance," Delano replied. Davis walked out of the room. Delano immediately made a quick check on the apartment, making sure it was not bugged. Certain that the room was safe he walked over to the thirty-two-inch LG plasma screen and switched it on.

He moved towards the couch and threw himself on it. After a moment, he picked up his luggage, opened it and brought out the parcel he neatly tucked away under the bottom of the bag. There was no inkling whatsoever that anything was hidden in his luggage; not even customs had been able to figure it out! Protected by an ultra-secret, sophisticated anti-metal detector.

He opened it and took out his favourite jack knife and the Colt 45 Rampant, a classic pistol of black steel trimmed in gold and white engraving on the stock at the front and back. It had a golden horse holding a white spear in its mouth, a golden safety and the handle walnut with golden screws with engraved spearheads facing each other. In its middle is a standing horse with a spear in its mouth, topped off with a stainless-steel trigger with three holes making it light for quick trigger action. His entire life as military personnel had depended on these tools, and they had fast become his best friends. This had gone unnoticed of course. Assembling the Colt 45 Rampant together, he polished it. The piece of metal was cool against his lips as he kissed it, and gently placed it under the cushion. He pulled off the white T-shirt he was wearing since he boarded the plane at the John F. Kennedy Airport in New York City. He folded it, and then lay down on the sofa with his hands behind his head. As he dozed off, a breaking news item flashed across the television screen.

"Welcome to Breaking News. A militant group fighting against the oil rich Niger Delta region allegedly kidnapped a U.S. Ambassador. In order to ensure the ambassador's rescue, the American government assigned one of its high-profile Marine officers, Delano Martin to the case," the news anchor reported. Delano looked for his picture, when it appeared on the screen, he jumped up from the couch. The news reporter continued, "We will bring you more information as the events leading to the rescue of the U.S. Ambassador unfold."

While Delano listened to the news, he heard a knock on the door. His eyes narrowed dangerously as he reached for his Colt 45 Rampant, and placed himself behind the door.

"Come on in!"

He waited for the door to swing open, and as it did, a female face came into view. The frightened woman stood tense, paralysed with fear. Delano lowered his gun and apologised to her.

"I'm sorry," he said, and as he closely examined the beautiful figure standing before him, his suspicion subsided. The room service girl, who had barely recovered from the shock of the gun pointed at her, spoke in a shaken voice.

"This parcel arrived a few minutes ago, and it has your room number written on it, so I brought it up to you." She handed over the parcel to him. Delano was surprised, because he had just arrived and knew no one.

"Parcel for me?" he asked enquiringly, as he hesitated for a while. He looked at the beauty before him, rubbed his cheek, smiled and collected the parcel from her.

The girl immediately turned to leave the room but Delano called her back. "Please, don't go." The girl stood still.

He searched his pocket and brought out a ten-dollar note from his pants pocket.

"Please, take this from me, a little tip."

The girl turned around to see the ten-dollar bill, and smiled her best smile. She took it from him and said, "Thank you, sir".

But before Delano could utter another word, she was gone. Delano yelled after her, "Maybe you should tell me your name?" The girl had disappeared. Smiling to himself, he rubbed his chin brusquely and walked to the refrigerator at the other end of the suite, opened it and perused its contents. He brought out a bottle of brewed soya milk and raised it up for inspection. Opening it, he took a long gulp from the bottle and sighed; it was a good sigh.

"This is beginning to look nice," he said to himself. After a long rejuvenating shower, he fell asleep promptly.

The window blinds flung open and the reflection of light fell on Delano's face. He tried to open his eyes, blinking several times as he shielded his face with his hand. Davis was standing by the bed.

"How did you get in here?" he asked wearily, still trying to make sense of what was happening.

"Who was here?" Davis asked suspiciously.

"No one Why?"

"You shouldn't ever leave your door open. We are late, the commissioner of police doesn't like to be kept waiting," replied Davis.

"What time is it?" asked Delano, rising up from the bed and removing the bed covers, revealing his well-built frame. He walked towards the bathroom.

"A few minutes to ten o'clock," replied Davis.

"Did you say ten?" Delano yelled from the bathroom.

"Yeah!" Davis shouted back.

"What is wrong with the sun in this part of the world? I'm burning up already!"

"Yeah, you are North of the equator," Davis wearily chipped in.

"Hope I survive this," he walked out of the bathroom, drying his hair with a towel, then got dressed. He wore a nice dark suit and a traditional bow tie.

"How do I look?" he asked.

Davis turned around and smiled, "Let's hit the road."

Delano smiled back and they headed out of the room.

The Commissioner of Police sat in his office, going through details in a file before him. A quick look at the office and judging from the memorabilia that adorned the wall, would tell a keen observer that he was a highly decorated officer of the Republic. He was reading the daily news with keen interest, like someone who had a PhD in Law, ready to defend. The harsh ringtone of the phone startled him. Annoyed, he snatched up the receiver and snarled into the earpiece.

"Commissioner of Police here."

The voice on the other line came out faintly. "Hello commissioner, this is the U.S. consulate attaché Patrick Astrid."

The Commissioner of Police changed his demeanour instantly into a friendly one as he answered the American attaché.

"Mr. Astrid, how are you?" the commissioner paused to listen. "Yes! I am expecting him any moment now. I know the task ahead," he answered appropriately. He listened again and continued. The Commissioner of Police replied, "Never mind, make sure he gets all he needs for his mission."

"Yes, we will definitely keep you informed," he replied and listened intently. The line on the other end went dead and the commissioner looked at the receiver in his hand. Fuming he hung up. He hated being bossed around! He was of the opinion that the twenty-eight years and more he spent in the Force were enough for everyone to accord him respect. He didn't like taking orders, an attitude that had led his subordinates to nickname him "No Face.", a term which illustrated a no-nonsense man. But ever since the kidnapping of the U.S. Ambassador, he became more or less a junior officer to the higher-ranking staff of other government agents and the American Consulate attaché who kept issuing orders to him. He hated the one and a half years which had refused to herald his retirement, an event he had been looking forward to for over twenty years! After all, he had lived a successful life in the Force.

He also felt comfortable with his achievements outside the Force. If not for the stipulations on retirement and the fanfare that went with it; especially the ceremonial parade, he would have chosen to resign peacefully to a quiet life with his family. But having paid his dues as an officer who had put in years of dedicated service and hard work in the Force, he was subject to greedy tendencies that would not allow him to resign. He savoured the accolades that were accorded to retiring senior officers. He believed he deserved his too. He returned his attention to his reading exercise, and before long he was rudely interrupted again by an abrupt knock on the door.

"What the hell is all this?" he cursed under his breath. "Can't I have a moment of peace? Come on in!" he shouted angrily.

The door opened and Davis walked in, followed by Delano. Upon seeing Delano, the demeanour of the commissioner changed again.

"Hey! My friend," he called out to Delano, and he stretched out his hand to him. "Sit down, sit down. How was your trip? Hope you are finding my country friendly?" A torrent of questions poured out. Delano just smiled. He couldn't really grasp what he was saying; his accent was a problem. Secondly, he didn't know which of the questions to answer first. He drew the only vacant chair in the office and sat down, while Davis was standing still, arms clipped to his side in the fashionable force tradition, a sign of respect shown by junior officers to their superiors.

"So, tell me, sir, these people, where do we find them? What are their motives? Are they asking for a ransom?" It was Delano's turn to pour out his questions in his American accent. The commissioner laughed.

"I guess Davis must have been filling you in with all the important details." A mischievous smile played around the commissioner's lips, the kind that showed disdain to a fast-tracking officer.

Delano strained his ear to hear him well. He smiled.

"Yea, not much though, I know," said the commissioner working with him. "If there is any other thing you would like to know concerning this situation?" the commissioner asked while he opened one of the files on his table and perused the contents, but not without ascertaining first that there was no implicating evidence in it. He pushed the file towards Delano.

"That will be of good help, son!" he said, smiling. Delano paid rapt attention to the first picture that stared up at him from the contents of the file.

"It is not much, but all the details on the activities of the kidnappers are in there." The commissioner's countenance changed to one of seriousness. "So when do you hope to start working?" he asked, his facial features hardening as he waited for his reply.

"What is this here?" asked Delano.

"What is what?" replied the commissioner, his mood changed. His swift gaze swept over Davis, who all this while had been maintaining his position behind Delano. He bent over to look at the photograph in Delano's hand. "Oh, that! It is an emblem of one of the many groups of the oil companies operating in the Republic," replied Davis as he returned to his position.

"Oh!" retorted the commissioner.

"So gentlemen, on one final note, we want to see results and end this issue on time. No delays will be accepted; no side tracking. Before you walked in, the American Consulate attaché called to make sure we will work as a team and rescue the U.S. Ambassador in no time. So gents, good luck." The Commissioner of Police concluded his farewell speech to them.

Delano stood up while Davis saluted the commissioner. They were about to leave, when the commissioner spoke again.

"Delano?"

Delano turned to face him.

"If there is anything that deserves my attention, my office will be open to you all hours."

"Thanks, I quite appreciate that, Mr commissioner," Delano responded and walked out. Davis followed suit. But as he was about to shut the door behind him, the commissioner called him back in.

"Davis?"

"Sir?" Davis answered and turned around and entered back into the office. The commissioner made a 'watch him' sign with his two fingers to his eyes. Davis nodded silently and walked out of the office.

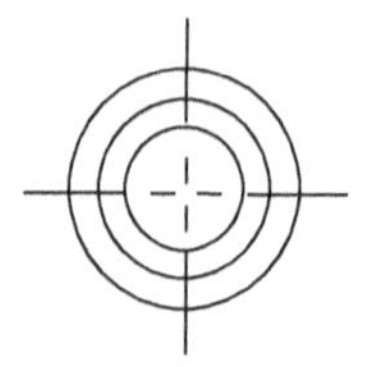

First Blood

Como walked through a narrow pathway overgrown with elephant grass. His destination was an abandoned building that lay on a waste land by the riverbank of the Oporozar river. He walked into the shattered building, which had recently been under constant attack from the Joint Task Force, because they surmised it was the hideout of the militants. Como was always lucky after coming here.

The Joint Task Force just left in their search for possible clues that could lead to the whereabouts of the kidnapped U.S. Ambassador. Their most pressing assignment at the moment was to clamp down on a small band of groups growing into militancy in the oil rich Niger-Delta region. The activities of a group of young militants agitated by the oil companies' development of their land were financed by suspected political powers. Enjoying political attention from the opposition, the militants played both sides of the greedy self-centred men on the verge of wresting political and financial power from the party ruling the country. But this directed attention to the development of the oil-rich area, leading to rumours that oil barons financed the vigorously aggressive acts of these militant groups. Government officers were also identified in the financing of the extreme violence of these new insurgent warlords, who had unleashed terror on the community. Como spoke deeply about the situation.

"Why kidnap a U.S. Ambassador, a man who has over the last few years fought against the slow pace of development in our land?"

Como was a heavily built, dark-skinned, man, the central commander of this renegade band of arms-carrying men. A self-proclaimed spiritual deity chose Como as a spiritual mouthpiece and the champion of the struggle for emancipation in the region. Como climbed up the shaky frame of the staircase that led to the first floor of what used to be a beehive of trading activities by the riverside, before it was knocked down by the Joint Task Force during one of their usual attacks. Killing unarmed civilians was an action that had often generated outrage and cries from both local and the international communities. The President had vowed to deal with these renegades by making sure that they would come to the table to discuss their grievances.

"It is either the table, or the gun" a spokesman on political matters once said in a press conference, as they had realised that there was a political undertone to the agitation.

"And if we do not nip their activities in the bud, then we will be allowing greedy politicians to overrun our land. Doing so would spell doom, not only for the Niger Delta, but for the entire country" the spokesman continued.

"Government action is to make sure we have a forum to discuss matters and know what the problem is. Killing and kidnapping won't solve the problem. The president has reaffirmed his resolve to establish stronger ties to bring the militants to the round table. And if this is not accepted by our brothers, then the Joint Force will be on them until they come to terms with the Government." That was the concluding statement of the spokesman. The conference elicited yet stronger criticism of the government for using the Force to kill innocent people.

Como meandered his way through a dark passage into a neatly-arranged room draped all over in white cloth. He took his seat at one end of the room and rested comfortably on the floor. Arms crossed over his chest, he swore in his native tongue, and immediately a thunderous sound took over the whole vicinity; a voice as forceful as the one depicted in the popular 'The Ten Commandments' movie, when Moses was given the commandments. The voice with a heavy accent echoed from nowhere and filled the hall.

"Worthy son, the generation yet unborn will remember you indefinitely for this fight that you have fought to liberate our land and our people from the degradation, poverty and death that have been imprinted on us for decades! The gods are happy, and they will always be with you." The voice echoed on.

"My ancestors there…," Como tried to say something, but he was interrupted by the voice.

"Unburden your heart, my son, for the white man you hear of, is not here to fight us, but to take that which belongs to him," Como remembered.

"What do we do then? For I fear for my people, their lives and properties, and poverty has become so rampant, and the death rate is getting out of hand," lamented Como.

"Send Unit II to follow him, for tomorrow they will come seeking the help of one of our very own," the voice paused and continued. "My son, the time for the truth has come; it is time." The echo of the voice was a strong, loud, sonorous sound, and then as swiftly as it had begun, it faded away. Como woke up with a start. Sweating profusely, he looked around and realised that he was still in his apartment.

"It was a dream," he murmured and paused for a moment with a wistful look on his face. "The gods spoke to me," he said again, as he kept pondering on the dream. His cell phone on the bedside close to his Beretta CX4 machine gun, started to ring. Como picked it up and looked at the time. It was fifteen minutes past the hour of two in the morning.

"Who can be calling me at this time of the night?" he asked rhetorically before he answered the call. He put the phone to his ear and the line went dead at the other end. He was startled.

"What is going on?" he wondered aloud. He immediately grabbed his walkie-talkie, and tried to reach out to the other boys. None of them answered.

"What is wrong? Where is everybody?" He paced up and down, wondering what this was all about. He walked to the window and raised the curtains. He then realised the heavy downpour outside, and lightning flashes and thunder bolts.

"Network problem," he reasoned. The lights went out and that only increased his frustration.

"Damn this country!" he cursed.

Using his lighter, he located the closest lamp and put it on, then went to the toilet to relieve himself.

Delano Martin was at a nightclub enjoying himself at a table by the bar. A young woman was dancing on the dance floor amidst other dancers. With a bottle of beer before him Delano watched with interest. His mind went down memory lane as he reminisced. She reminded him of Janice. Janice Karen, a dark-skinned black woman Delano had run into while in his final semester in college. There was chemistry between the two of them and they had wasted no time in getting to know each other. The fruit of the relationship was Delano Martin Junior. Before Janice, Delano lived a reckless life, which left a huge scar on his heart, love and his relationships.

The superintendent at the State Department helped him to get his life back on track. One summer morning Delano was taking his family out for a picnic. The 2007 Dodge they had been driving skidded off the road and flipped. The eyewitnesses on the scene immediately called 911. Nevertheless, it was too late. Right before his very eyes, his most cherished possessions died. Watching the young woman dance, practically brought memories of Janice back into his mind.

"You like her?" a voice asked. It was Inspector Davis keeping his eyes on Delano. He took a seat, eyes fixed on the dancing woman.

"I see there are a handful of attractive beauties in this stunning landscape," Delano simply replied.

"I bet you can say that again! She can be yours," Davis added, as he winked at him. Inspector Davis got up from his stool and walked through the dancing crowd towards the woman. Reaching for her, Davis whispered into her ear. The girl giggled as her eyes trailed in the direction where Delano was sitting and watching them. Davis walked back to meet him. Delano thought about Janice Karen, she had been Med Student. The two of them established a relationship after meeting at a fundraising ceremony for People Living with HIV-AIDS (PLWHA).

At that moment, three men came into the club. All dressed in white suits, they walked towards the bar. As one of them turned around, the girl on the dance floor seemed to recognise them and she froze in fear. Delano, who was enjoying every bit of the young woman's act, noticed that her countenance had changed. He turned and looked around, and noticed the three men. Had they been on her trail for some reason, he silently wondered. Turning round again, he noticed the young woman had vanished. Immediately he walked out of the club and into the street. He looked left and right and saw nobody. He followed his police instincts and walked in the right direction.

Davis, who had left him sitting at the bar, returned and did not see him. He took a quick scan of the floor of the club and noticed that the young woman was gone too.

"It is natural," Davis muttered smiling to himself and walked out of the club house. Going straight to the top floor of the hotel where Delano was staying, Davis knocked on the door and waited. No answer. He knocked and banged on the door, still no answer.

He peeped through the keyhole. There was no sign of anybody. Immediately he ran in search of Delano. Davis stood on the street; he looked at both sides, puzzled and worried. He started running on a path looking for Delano. Davis ran for half a mile until he got to the next junction. Inspector Davis was standing contemplating where to go next, when he saw Delano walking towards him.

"What happened?" Davis asked.

"She walked into the street, I looked away for a second and she disappeared," he replied wearily.

"Of course, they come from the streets and they go back to the streets," Davis said on a lighter note to cheer Delano up.

"She is in trouble," Delano added, wondering where she was right now.

Delano was still not looking happy, and his eyes darted from one side of the road to the other, apparently looking for her. Davis looked at him with some reservation as they walked on. The two cops rolled in the Peugeot 406 and parked under the tail of tall trees and grown grasses.

"What are we doing here?" asked Delano as they came out of the car.

"This is the crime scene, where the convoy was double crossed" he said to Delano. They walked around, looking for some more clues. Delano saw some expended cartridges. He bent down and picked them up.

"Yes! Here are some guns!" Inspector Davis shouted. This drew Delano's attention.

"How did these weapons get to this place? They are from Russia. The last experience I had with these weapons was in Afghanistan," Delano said surprised.

"They are brought in by smugglers, oil smugglers, who destroy oil facilities and sabotage the activities of the government and oil companies," Davis answered.

"Smugglers?" he exclaimed.

"How do they pay for them; I mean the locals?"

"They exchange them with stolen crude oil from the destroyed oil facilities of the multinationals," Davis answered and moved away, as he cleverly avoided Delano's question. Both men walked through the overgrown bush path. After a mile, they got to the bank of the creek. Delano awed by the sight of the beautiful landscape.

"What beauty!" he exclaimed.

"I see the reason for the waterway projects, this scenery is spectacular," Delano said, taking in the scenery.

"Yeah, I guess so. There." Davis pointed ahead to the horizon.

"That was the escape route, across the cliff," he said, pointing towards the dense mangrove on the other side of the river.

"So why is it so difficult to get there? Demolish the goddamn hole, and smoke out this handful of rodents," Delano said. His language infuriated Davis, who looked at him with disdain.

"Hey, did I say something wrong?" Delano asked.

Davis walked on, with Delano following him. A few minutes before five, the Peugeot 406 drove into the Divisional Police headquarters. They both get out and walked into the building. They walked past an officer abusing a suspect.

"What is he doing?" Delano inquired.

"Interrogation," Davis answered briefly. Delano shook his head pathetically.

"Oh my, what a way to interrogate someone!" Delano sighed.

Delano followed Davis as they enter the corridor of the precinct. They headed for the office of Adedotun Akintola, the Commissioner of Police. His secretary informed them that the commissioner would not be meeting them in his office.

"Where can we meet him? We want to give the morning report," Inspector Davis said.

"He is conducting the day meeting in the main meeting hall," the secretary replied.

"This way," Davis instructed Delano. They headed out, and come to a big double door.

Inside the room, seven senior officers of the Force were seated. Their gaze fell on Inspector Davis and Delano Martin as they entered the main meeting hall's entrance.

Inspector Davis greeted them. So did Delano with a nod of the head. The silence was oppressive. Everyone seemed cautious of the stranger. The Commissioner of Police tried desperately to smile, when Inspector Davis walked up to him and whispered in his ear. The commissioner nodded.

"Well done men," he said.

Davis walked close to Delano who maintained a standing position. After a while, Inspector Davis said, "Let's go!"

When they were about to leave, Delano remembered something.

"Hey!" Delano said turning and heading back to the table where he placed the expended cartridges he had collected from the abduction site.

"Nice piece." Dropping it on the table, Delano ran to catch up with Davis. The ranking officers all looked at one another with puzzled expressions on their faces. It was the commissioner who broke the silence with a cough.

"Can this Delano be trusted commissioner?" one of the senior officers asked.

"He can. After all, he reports all his findings to me. And Davis will be on him all the way, so gentlemen, there is no reason to fear Delano," the commissioner said.

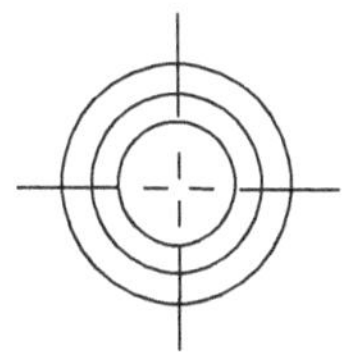

The Brotherhood

The oil barons were a few powerful Nigerian businessmen. Their involvement in the oil-rich environment of the country made them powerful. They controlled everything in the high, public and private business sectors within and outside the Republic. Their network spanned Europe, the Americas, the Caribbean Islands, and recently, with the advent of the Internet, the Asian tigers had become their new allies. Until the kidnapping of the U.S. Ambassador, their activities had been very successful, especially with the lucrative triangle established by their rulers within the region. The local police force enjoyed bribes, hush money and pay-offs, the windfall from these big oil companies. The oil barons successfully sponsored political office holders and members of parliament. The politicians helped setup the arms and drug imports, their influence in the Republic was overwhelming. The new area for gun-running was in the oil rich Niger-Delta region. These guns were then used to sponsor political thuggery before and during elections. With the agitation for the development of the region, these guns had become instruments the barons now feared would destroy them. The kidnapping of the U.S. Ambassador was therefore something they strongly criticised, as it increased the involvement of the American government.

The issue of not trusting Delano was one that had emerged from the conviction that Americans were schemers, who loved taking advantage of every situation, even if it damaged existing relationships. It was late in the evening, and after a hectic day's work of moving around, familiarising himself with the recent details, and getting to know the geographical terrain, Delano took a hot bath and decided to rest. He sat on the sofa and stared blankly at the television, drinking from a bottle of Soya milk; a drink he found greatly refreshing since he first had a taste of it, a few days ago. He was deep in thought. The soft sounds of the lyrics from "A Rose is Still a Rose." by Aretha Franklin, drifted from the Home Theatre; a tune Delano always listened to whenever thoughts of Janice flooded his mind. As he listened to the soft tunes, Delano heard a knock on the door. At first, he ignored it. But then again, the knock continued in a series of hard and heavy knocks. Jumping from the couch, he picked up his companion, his Colt 45, and looked at the time. It was fifteen minutes before midnight. Pointing the gun at the door, he inched close to it and on the spur of the moment had a second thought.

"The room service woman. Could she be the person?" he muttered to himself. "I wouldn't want to scare her again today." A hundred and one thoughts of what to do were raging in his head when he heard the loud knock again. This time he edged to the door and flung it open and there stood the young woman who had vanished into the night at the club the previous evening.

"They are after me!" she said crying as she stumbled into the room, brushing him aside. Delano took a quick look through the hallway. Certain that nobody had followed, he closed the door behind him and walked over to meet the visibly-shaking woman. "Who are these people?" he asked. The woman sat mute on the couch, unable to say a word. He looked at her, and imagined what she must have gone through.

"I will be back." Delano walked across the room, hopped into his pants and went into the kitchen. He made a quick cup of coffee and handed it to the young woman. She looked at it and declined.

"You no get any food for here?" She asked him in the fashionable Nigerian Pidgin English. A slang Delano had enjoyed since his arrival in the country and had heard the locals speak.

"What?" Delano stuttered.

"I mean food, I am hungry."

"Hungry? I haven't got any damn food in here."

"Then do something," she said.

"Like what?"

He mulled her request for less than a second, then said "Ok. I will be right back." He walked to the phone and dialled a number. There was no answer. He dropped the receiver and walked back to the young woman.

"One minute, please," he told her, and then left the room. Certain that it was safe outside the hall, Delano hurried away and got to the reception. He called out and waited, but there was no reply. He looked around, but the place was empty and he wondered where everybody had gone. Delano saw a narrow corridor and decided to try it, and to his great dismay, he discovered the body of a young woman lying in a pool of blood. He quickly moved and bent over her. It was the room service lady he had wanted to see again! Delano examined her but she was already dead. He was looking for a clue, when he saw a shadow flash past.

Anxiously springing to his feet, he slowly and cautiously went through the stairs that led back to his room again. But when he opened the door of the room, the young woman was gone. Delano rushed through the broken window seeing movements at the foot of the building. He heard the young woman screaming. Swiftly, he climbed over the window sill and dropped down on the grassy lawn and went after them. He ran left, along the fence of the hotel, following the sound of the screaming young woman. He turned right and saw a hole in the fence, and he walked through it.

Delano ran for several miles, not knowing where he was and then he realised the screaming had stopped. Delano took a moment to figure out which way to follow. Looking around, he decided to continue to run along the path. He tripped, stumbled and fell. As he rolled over landing with his Colt 45 Rampant in hand, Delano crawled quietly toward the figure that lay there. To his utter amazement, it was the young woman! Her throat was cut and gushing blood. But she was still alive. Immediately he tore off a part of his pants, tied up the wound and carefully carried the young woman, who was trying desperately to say something to him.

"Don't worry, you will be alright," he said. Delano ran with the woman in his arms and came to a road normally busy but deserted on that particular night.

He looked around; at that moment he was confused and felt lost. He headed towards the road with the body, hoping to see anybody in a car or a Good Samaritan, failing to realise that he was thousands of miles from New York City where vehicles are around even in the dead of night. He stood there, holding the woman, wondering what to do next. A flash of blinding light from across the road bathed him and the dying young woman in its rays. Delano strained his eyes to see who it was, and saw a man wearing a police uniform. He immediately recognised him as a law enforcement officer.

"Thank goodness," he muttered. "Officer, officer!" he shouted as he carried the young woman's body with the utmost care.

"Please, this is an emergency!" he screamed. "She needs urgent medical attention."

They walked close to each other. "Wetin happen, wetin happen?" The police officer saw the young woman covered in blood. The cop became scared and step back momentarily.

"Hold am dere!" the officer said. Delano did not understand what he said but moved towards him, his instincts telling him he was in deep trouble.

The officer sounded his whistle to alert the other officers planted in the dark, where they had their road block mounted.

"Murderer, Murderer!" shouted the first officer. Delano still struggled to lift the lifeless body of the young woman that lay on the ground and tried to give them explanations but to no avail. They rounded up Delano and handcuffed him. Suddenly, a police van appeared out of nowhere, they forced him in and drove away.

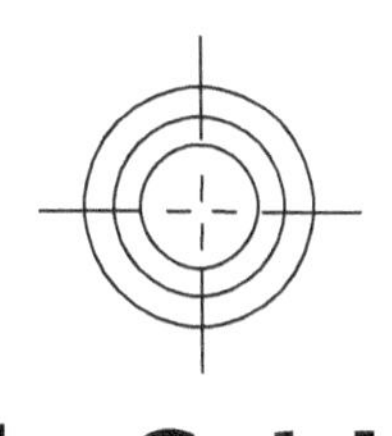

The Set-Up

It was in the early hours of the morning; the commissioner had slept soundly in the warm embrace of his beloved wife of thirty-five years. He was grateful that the responsibility of finding and rescuing the kidnapped U.S. Ambassador, had been shifted to Delano. He hadn't had a moment like this with his wife in a long time. She had suggested over time that he resign from the Force and enjoy a peaceful life and spend time with her, especially now that her health was failing rapidly. She needed him more than ever now as their kids were all grown up and had left home. She suffered from osteoporosis, a condition that was taking a toll on her. The doctor had advised her to engage in more physical exercise during the day. That was the reason why she needed his company more than ever; although there was little he could do, especially as he was getting older, and the children were far away from home. Their eldest son, James, was in the United States pursuing a career in criminology, a course influenced by his father's successful life on the Force. Junior was in Malaysia. He settled for Information Technology Networking and Programming, as his early contact with modern electronics engineering, and the revolution in telecommunications in the developing world was a lucrative business, which had influenced the choice of his career. Betty, the oldest of the three, was currently enjoying blissful married life with her husband in England, UK, where they had been for over ten years. Despite the repeated cries of loneliness his wife had uttered, her desire to see her grandchildren had fallen on deaf ears. The continued political and socio-economic downturn of Nigeria had become a pretext for couples not to come back home. The insecurity problem was another issue currently plaguing the country, one which the militant activities had posed in recent times.

The beep of his mobile phone woke the commissioner up. He ignored the first call. But the repeated ringing of the phone could only mean one thing "trouble". Grudgingly, he snapped open his phone, and heard a glut out of words at the other end. That brought him back to full consciousness. He heard a white America was in their custody for the murder of a young woman. The commissioner's eyes widened in surprise and snapped.

"I am sending someone down!" He made the call and promptly went back to sleep.

Delano and Davis walked down the hall of the jail cell and got out of the building. Delano looked tired, scruffy and dirty. "What happened to the young woman?" was Delano's first question. Davis ignored it. They got into the vehicle waiting for them, and drove off. Delano still insisted on knowing what happened to the young woman. Delano kept bombarding Davis with that question, who became irritated with him.

"You stink, man, you need a bath," Davis simply said.

"I don't need a bath, all I want to do right now is to see that woman," Delano shouted.

"The young woman is dead!" Davis hollered back at him "Are you satisfied now?"

"I want her, dead or alive," Delano retorted.

"Don't bother about that. The Commissioner of Police is waiting to see you at the office." Davis drove on.

"What mother fucking country is this? You people take delight in death! No protection from the law enforcement agents! And nobody seems to want to know what happens to the poor."

His ranting was ignored by Davis, whose main focus was to get him cleaned up and take him to see the commissioner, who apparently was expecting them at the office. The Commissioner of Police was livid as he paced up and down his office silently. The only thing on his mind was his retirement day which was nowhere in sight! Everything seemed to be falling out of shape. The Commissioner of Police thought Delano's arrival would make things easy but with the recent events, he feared what would happen next. His mind pondered on the rescue mission. The Commissioner of Police didn't know when he started to talk out loud to himself.

"Why can't those Americans mind their own business? We didn't say we could not rescue the U.S. Ambassador, so why did they have to send one of their own into this?" he paused and paced again.

"Delano!" he yelled. He barely sat down, when Davis knocked on the door and walked into the office with Delano. Seeing Delano, the commissioner exploded. "Your indulgence has led to the death of a man and that of an innocent young woman!"

"My indulgence? Guess you should have expected him to kill me too!" replied Delano.

"He came after the woman, not after you! And by the way, what was it you were doing with a whore in your hotel room?" the commissioner shouted back at him.

"I won't stand here to be insulted. And you don't tell me who to be with, and when or where! It's my damn life!" Delano yelled back. The war of words raged on.

"Your 'damn life' is to save the U.S. Ambassador, not to run after club women," snapped the commissioner.

Delano clenched his fists at his sides. "One more word from your damn fucking mouth and I'm going to break your damn neck!" And Delano moved into position to make good on his promise to the commissioner. Davis shifted uncomfortably and knew he had to intervene fast.

"Sir…," Inspector Davis started but the office phone rang and interrupted him. The commissioner snapped up the receiver and hollered, "Hello?"

He heard the voice of the ambassador from the Consulate's office on the other end and brought down his pitch. "Good morning, sir," the commissioner said with a frown on his face. "Yes sir…OK sir." He handed the phone to Delano, who snatched it from him angrily.

"Good morning, sir," Delano said "Yes, I am fine…OK… I was supposed to visit the village." He dropped the phone and stormed out of the office.

The commissioner looked at Davis. "Keep to the plan," he said, "Don't allow him to get close to any evidence."

"Yes sir," Davis answered and left the office.

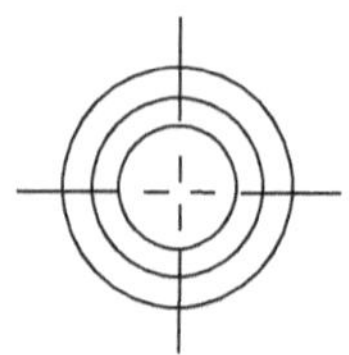

An Unusual Friend

Delano took an angle inside a diner called Domino's, along the double lane airport road by the Ajamimogha junction. He remembered having a sumptuous meal there once with Davis during one of their investigations for clues. Davis had once told him that at times the militants did come around to lavish their loot on girls, food and drinks after a hit. His best bet was to come and see if, by any chance, the man who had attacked and killed the girl would come around, if what Davis said was really true about the outlet serving as a payment point for marksmen. If his assailant was a marksman, as his instincts told him, then he would definitely come here to be paid off for last night's job he pulled off in the hotel room.

Delano sat there, drinking his Gulder beer, a drink he had fallen in love with. It had taken Davis over an hour though to convince him of the fine taste of the drink at the club the night he met the dead woman. Delano was watching each and every man who passed through the door when his phone rang. It was Davis. He refused to take the call, but called to the bar attendant and ordered yet another drink. It would be his fourth bottle. He liked it when he drank this much. He once told Janice before their marriage, when she had almost broken up with him because of his drinking. He told her that it brought out the detective instincts in him, making him better prepared to handle even the vilest of situations. But now that he found himself in a different clime, he was compelled to go back to his former way of discovering the clues which escaped him. The situation he found himself in totally eluded the basic security norms known all over the world. He remembered in the Middle-East and Sudan where, despite the high rate of crime and insecurity, the lives of the citizens were held in high esteem, he still couldn't fathom why the

Police Force could just allow that innocent young lady to die, when she had a fifty-fifty chance of survival. It was one thing he could not come to terms with, and something deep inside him told him that it was not a coincidence, rather it was a justification for someone trying to sabotage the mission to the Republic. He felt his head spin; the effect of the alcohol was gradually taking a toll on his brain. He was recalling the young woman's first words that hit him hard.

"They want to kill me." Her words kept echoing in his head. He was desperately trying to clear his mind, when he saw a man come into the eatery. He became alert and watched stealthily, as the man who had just walked in was welcomed by another one who came out from an inner office. He knew he couldn't miss the figure he saw twice that night. He became suspicious, and watched them closely. Both men walked back into the inner office.

Delano called the bar attendant, who attended to him again. Bringing out some of the Naira notes he changed days before, he handed a few to pay him. Then he settled to watch any suspicious move that might come from the office. He became restless and impatient, when suddenly his mobile phone rang again. This time he answered the call.

"Yeah Nigger," Delano blurted out as he listened to Davis while watching every move in the diner. "The one on the outskirt of town. Domino's, I think."

Davis could be heard in the background, "Ok, will be with you in the next thirty minutes."

"Thirty minutes is a long time to solve some of this mystery," Delano said to himself as he waited. Then all of a sudden, a man about five feet, seven inches tall walked up to him. The wrinkles on his face showed that he was over fifty years old. Floating in an oversize black suit, he looked frail and dirty, and dusty old shoes adorned his feet. He had very unkempt hair, and a thick beard. He drew out a chair and sat before him. Delano answered Davis' last words on the phone.

"Ok I'll be waiting," Delano said looking directly at the man, and he introduced himself as a journalist from one of the national newspapers.

"Can I help you?" Delano asked the journalist, who carelessly threw some photographs at him. Delano took a quick look. Surprise crept on his face as he saw the photo of the dead woman with the policemen the night she was killed.

"Where did you get these?" he asked.

"I think you should be asking what will happen to you next," replied the strange-looking man.

Delano was puzzled. "What do you mean what will happen to me next?"

The journalist ignored his question. "My friend, you are about to be deported back to the States, and that is not something you want to experience right now. One look at you shows that you are getting into something you can't finish."

Delano cut him off abruptly. "Who are you, and what do you want?"

"Just a friend; and as for what I want?" He paused and thought for a while. "Some truth."

"Truth?" asked Delano, "What truth?"

The journalist looked around the whole place. Certain that everything was right, he leaned forward and whispered, "I can't tell you here. The only thing that might interest you now is that those who want to send you packing are almost here."

Delano stared at him.

"You have less than five minutes to come with me. We have spent twenty-five minutes out of the thirty minutes. Davis will be here soon." When he heard these words, Delano's eyes popped. But at that precise instant his attention was drawn to the two men whom he had previously seen, walking out of the office. The host bid the guest good-bye and the rest left. Delano noticed he was carrying a bag, which Delano suspected to be money.

The journalist spoke, "Delano, I think it would be better to save your energy for the time being." He hadn't finished what he was about to say, when they heard the sound of police sirens in the distance. The journalist stood up. He gathered the photos together from the table.

"Follow me, if you wish to find the U.S. Ambassador."

He quickly walked out of the diner. Delano did not hesitate, and followed him outside. They entered the Volkswagen GTI 4 parked outside, and drove off. Davis arrived with men from the Police Force. The host who had just walked back into his office came in again to welcome him. Unaware that Delano had left, he pointed to the direction he was sitting. He was surprised to see that the table was empty. He asked the service boys at the bar counter.

"Where is the American that was sitting over there?" They all shrugged their shoulders and replied, "We don't know."

"Men, let's go!" Davis walked out. He took out his phone and made a call as they get into the car. The voice came through the receiver.

"Target is nowhere to be found. Mission now in intense pursuit." The car drove into the distance.

The creaky door opened to reveal the dark interior of the house. The journalist and Delano walked inside. Delano, who did not know where he was or who he ran away with, waited patiently. The journalist finally laid his hand on the match box he was looking for. He lit the kerosene lamp on top of the television set. The yellow flame lit up the interior. He walked into one of the rooms, leaving Delano standing there. Delano took a look at the gross surroundings of the house, and found out that they were inside a mud hut. Posters covered the great part of the hut, displaying figures of both local and foreign politicians. He could recognise the faces of past and recent American Presidents. The other photos he saw though, he didn't know anything about. He guessed that they were important to the man, a man whom he barely knew. As he looked around, he saw a photograph of himself at the airport on the day he arrived in the country. Beside it was the photo of him looking at the dead woman. While he wondered who his host was, he had a flashback of the young woman dancing at the club. He remembered seeing a faded tattoo on her shoulder the night she had walked into his room. Walking closer to the poster, he looked intently at the tattoo on the shoulder of the woman's photograph on the wall. His host returned, carrying a bottle of beer and a bottle of gin. He handed the beer to Delano.

"Where the hell do these come from?" he asked, as he saw that it was a foreign drink he had been given and he took it.

"Drink, my friend."

They cheered, and Delano took his seat on one of the cane chairs of the hut.

"These pictures, where do they come from, and how did you get them?" Delano asked his unfamiliar host. The journalist drank the gin straight from the bottle, standing up. He staggered a little, smiled, and walked over to a bag hanging on the wall over an old Television set. He dipped his hand into the bag and retrieved a Kodak Kodamatic 960 Instant camera, then walked back to his seat. Delano carefully watched his every move, as everything he did became suspicious. The man placed the camera on the table.

"My baby, my most prized possession. He sees everything."

"Who are you?" Delano inquired.

"Sorry, let me formally introduce myself to you." He smiled. Delano looked at him. The man, who sat upright on the chair, stretched his hand to shake Delano's. Delano hesitated for a few seconds, not knowing what this freaky fellow was up to. He sized him up, and thought in his mind.

"If he does anything funny, I'm going to break his neck." He knew that the man couldn't match his strength. He was wary. He heard and read a lot about the Voodoo practices of black people in tropical Africa, and thought that a fellow like this, who looked so weird, could be one of such people, especially judging from the little he had been told on his arrival here about the mystical prowess of the militants. He didn't want to be caught off guard by this unusual friend. He looked at him, hand still stretched. He decided to gamble at his chance of being alive. He shook the man's hand. The journalist burst out laughing he grabbed Delano's hand. Delano got hold of his hand in a firm grip, expecting the next move. The journalist laughed uncontrollably. Seeing the frail figure before him, Delano could not help but join in the mirth. They laughed until they could laugh no more.

Still gasping for breath, the journalist said, "I am Preye, an undercover journalist. I have been following the story of this region for the past forty-five years."

"Forty-what!?" exclaimed Delano. He tried to figure out his age. At forty-five, he remembered, his father was already an accomplished man. He managed everything for his son before his death. He looked at Preye, and could understand the challenges he must have gone through as a private investigating journalist. His contemporaries back in the States lived in luxury. Preye stood up again and went over to the bag hanging above the television set. He returned with a memo pad, dusted it and opened it. He started reading without considering whether or not Delano was listening. But, of course, he was listening, as he did not want to miss anything this unusual friend was about to pass to him. Isaac Adaka Boro had been the first of his peers to speak up against the oppression the people of the region had faced before 1965, when he became aware of the injustices they were exposed to from oil explorations. Today he was an unsung hero, whom nobody recognised. He was seen as a rebel by those whose oppressive power had silenced the people for a long time.

The agitation of the people had become a taboo not to be mentioned. For over fifty years, the region had suffered poverty. Preye paused and watched the man in front of him.

"The oil companies that traverse the vast lands of the region endanger lives and properties," he continued. "The ruling elite, instead of paying attention to the cries for development of the people within the region, have carted away billions of dollars into Swiss banks." He paused and flipped over some pages of the memo he was reading from, straining his eyes. Delano looked at him, Preye was trying hard to decipher what was written on the memo.

The gin had gradually taken its toll on him. He cleared his voice and spoke once again.

"Every year, billions of dollars are taken from this region and used to build and develop other regions, while the people here suffer the results of wasted lands, and food shortages. No care or attention is given to them."

Picking up the bottle of the locally brewed gin, he gulped some more of its contents. Clearing his voice again, he went on reading, but he now struggled with his pronunciations.

"It was the Ogonis who first spoke out about the deplorable state of their farmlands and water, which was their only means of livelihood. A son of the soil fought and died for the cause, for the development of their land."

"How did he die?" Delano, who now sat quietly and seemed captivated by the story, looked at Preye expecting an answer.

"He was hanged. His body was dumped and bathed in acid solution by the military junta of the now late dictator General Sani Abacha, who inflicted untold suffering and hardship on the whole nation during his reign." He flipped over some more pages of his memo and brought out the picture of a man with an inscription.

"Is there any problem?" he asked, seeing the worried look on Delano's face.

"Wiwa." Preye showed the photo to him, and took a deep breath pouring some more gin into his mouth. Delano, who had hardly gulped down his first bottle of beer because he already had enough at the diner, looked at him. His gaze passed over his wrist watch. He saw the hand of the clock ticking towards midnight.

"Worried about sleeping?" Preye asked. Delano looked at the frail figure before him, wondering the secret of his strength. Three quarters of the gin bottle was gone, and he barely moved.

"The task ahead is not for the weak. You are a US Marine, if I am not mistaken. I have read as a young boy in college how you, Marines, are "invincible" in the course of your mission. So my friend, drink, for tomorrow may not be so pleasant."

"Not pleasant? Why?" Delano inquired.

"They are coming to get you, but don't worry, he will protect you; only if you will listen to him."

"Who is he and what business do I have with him? I am here to get the U.S. Ambassador and get the heck out of this hell hole!" Delano spat out.

"Not so fast, not so fast," Preye said despairingly, with a shaky voice.

"After the death of Ken-Saro Wiwa, a new group of young men, empowered by hungry, uncultured and power-thirsty politicians, re-surfaced." Delano listened with rapt attention on the new subject matter.

"These are the ones that have morphed into what they now call militants."

"What is their interest?" Delano asked, intensely looking at Preye, whose voice had become drowsy. Preye's eyes gradually closed. "The fight for economic regeneration, social empowerment, political involvement, and the structural development of. the hens that lay the golden eggs, and, and…," he answered, yawning, as he struggled to say more.

Delano dipped his hand into his denim pocket and brought out the expended cartridges of the bullets collected at the kidnapping site.

"And where do all these come from?" he inquired again, curious to know what weapons he was expected to see.

"That?" Preye yawned, ignoring the piece of metal placed on the table crowded with books. "From Europe, Russia, America and the Middle-East from merchants and barons who are involved in the big oil business, sponsored by greedy multinationals, who are disguising as messiahs for the local community, but have set the people in harm's way with the government."

Preye continued, "These smugglers, some of them are our fellow-citizens. They are the ones giving us a bad image. They exchange the weapons for crude oil. The weapons are smuggled at high sea and oil facilities locations, which usually cause the spillages that have affected the environment."

"Crude oil?" Delano asked in surprise.

"Yes, crude oil, one of the finest in the world. Those barons who are behind the cartel…," he started to say but at this point Delano stood up and walked from his chair to the poster bearing the dancing girl's image. He pointed to the oil dropping tattoo on her shoulder, "What is this all about? I have seen it before."

"That, I can't tell you," Preye replied weakly. Delano gazed at the half-sleeping man. He walked to him, shook him to wake him up, and looked into his eyes.

"I have to know. I think the girl was about to tell me something. I have a feeling it has to do with the kidnapping of the U.S. Ambassador."

Preye opened his eyes and looked at him. Closing them again, he managed to say in a faint voice, "To - moor - row." And then he slept off.

It was as if the lamp waited for Preye to sleep. It started blinking, showing signs of lack of kerosene. Delano watched the two figures, one peacefully asleep and the other in a dance posture on the poster. He stood up, walked to the poster and looked at the girl intently. As he rubbed his hand on the photograph, the lamp went off.

Matchsticks were struck. Preye was up already. He located the kerosene lamp on top of the television set and lit it. Yellow flames brightened up the hut, but then the lamp started to blink again.

"No. Not now!" he cried out. He moved towards Delano, who was still sleeping on the chair, and rocked him, "Time to go." The lamp went off again.

The two of them barely saw each other in the fresh light at dawn which pierced through the holes on the palm fronds used to roof the hut.

"What time is it?" Delano asked.

"Four a.m. We must leave now. The daylight must not find us here. It is not safe. By now, they must have found out we are here."

Delano protested, "I must go back. I have to find the U.S. Ambassador. I am grateful for all the assistance, hope to see you again," Delano's voice echoed in the still dark hut.

"Then you will either rot in jail, or in a graveyard. Or at best be sent back to the States, and the U.S. Ambassador, you will never see again. This is the Republic, not America! As for the dead woman, I mean the young woman you killed..."

Delano cut him off at once. "I didn't kill any one!"

"My friend, you are not in the States. You have murdered someone, and the only way to free yourself is to come with me, that is, if you want to stay alive and accomplish your mission."

Preye swiftly opened the door, and the cold morning air blew on his face. He relished the pleasure of the sensation. If there was anything Preye enjoyed in his self-imposed profession, it was the coolness of the morning dew that bathed him every time he left his place. Making sure that the environment was safe, he called Delano.

"Let's go!" He walked out into the field of dew drenched grass that surround the hut. Delano had no choice but to follow him. They took a few strides from the hut and turned into a path overgrown still with dewy grass and pressed on.

Delano dipped his hand into the pocket of his jacket and brought out a compass. He checked it, and said to Preye, "We are heading towards the sea."

"We are indeed," the other replied, as he walked on, not paying attention to him.

"We must arrive before sunrise. They are waiting for us."

"Us...Who are they?" Delano insisted, as bewilderment filled his mind.

"Be patient, my friend. It is said that the vulture is a patient bird, one virtue you must learn to develop on this mission."

They moved on along the path. A cold breeze engulfed them.

"We are close."

Suddenly Delano dived and pulled his companion to the ground. "Down!" he hissed.

As they fell on the ground, gunshots exploded near hem. Delano swiftly rolled over and crawled in the grass, his Colt 45 Rampant in hand. Preye squatted opposite him, pistol in hand too. Footsteps were heard from different directions. Delano immediately counted the movements. Gesturing to Preye, he indicated. 'Three of them'. The two men fired in the direction of the militants, then they perceived the sound of bodies falling to the ground in the distance. Preye heard the faint roaring of a PT-90 becoming audible. "They are here, this way!"

He ran for the sea. Delano followed. Groups of militants wearing face masks and military style camouflage appeared, holding assault rifles. The boat came to a halt before them. Preye looked at the boat and immediately noticed that it was different from those of the

Guerrilla units.

"Crocodile!" he cried.

"We have been double-crossed!"

As the boat glided to a steady halt, the militants surrounded them with their assault weapons. A fierce-looking man at the head of the boat ordered them.

"Drop your weapons and come with us!"

Preye obeyed and moved into the boat. Delano hesitated.

The man repeated, "American, drop your weapon!"

Immediately, four of the militants jumped off the boat. Sensing their mood, Delano dropped his Colt 45 and walked over to them. As he was getting on board, the rest of the militants jumped back into the boat. Their pursuers came out from the surrounding vegetation and saw them in the boat. Satisfied, they walked in the water and climbed in as well. Then they all glided away on the sea.

As they disappeared into the distance, behind them, from the opposite direction, the Crocodile roared into view. The occupants saw the boat gliding away with Preye and Delano.

"We have been double-crossed," one of the militants cried out helplessly watching the boat speed along the waterways and head out of sight.

The Unit

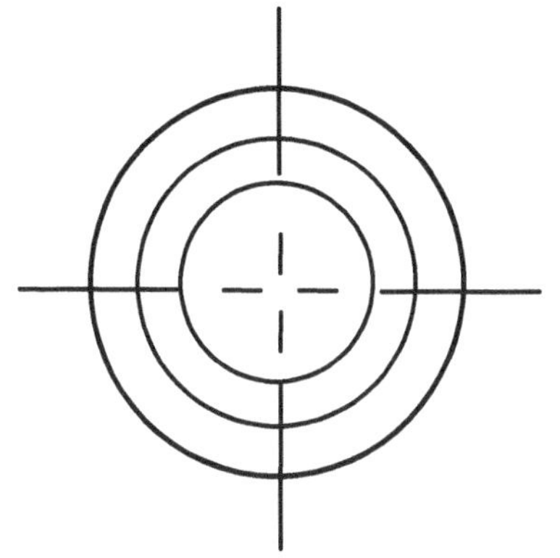

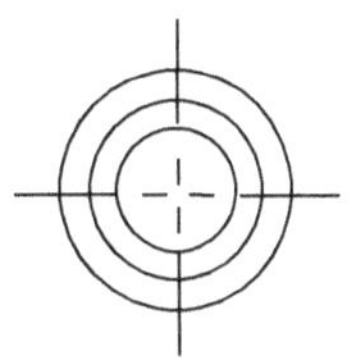

The Unit

The Ambassador and his subordinates were worried about the sudden disappearance of Delano. Efforts had been intensified within the combined Forces over the last forty-eight hours to try to locate Delano's whereabouts, but all to no avail. There was a report on the radio from an eye witness who had testified seeing some militants take him hostage, kill him, and throw his corpse into the water at high tide. A naval team had been mandated to search and find the remains of his body. They vigorously did this for twenty-four hours, not that it mattered much, since such events are commonly perpetuated within the region and nobody cared. Various foreign governments had supported the action of the federal forces.

Some of them had even claimed that the involvement of their nationals in the smuggling within the creeks was in no way connected to their respective countries. They even insinuated that those arrested or killed within the creeks were impostors who used the names of their claimed countries for nefarious activities. The government of the Republic was thus exonerated in cases of such killings. But this particular case in question was one that could not have been brushed aside just like the others, as the American government and other world leaders, including governmental institutions, were interested. The government of the United States was growing impatient with the activities of the militants in the creek. It had been concluded that their activities contributed to the dropping of world energy demand, which worsened the effect of the global recession faced by almost all the European and American economies. An action that had cast a doubt on the re-election of the American President to the White House. Barrels of crude supplies over the world skyrocketed and called for the government to intensify efforts to bring the activities of these groups to an end. The government of the Republic was leaving no stone unturned in trying to find a lasting solution to the militancy problem through dialogue and counter dialogues, offering to grant amnesty in exchange for weapons, and reabsorbing the people concerned back into the framework of society. It was in the wake of the offer of amnesty that the U.S. Ambassador had been kidnapped, and now it was an agent. The problem was evolving into a large-scale war. And if it was allowed to fully break out, the Republic could not withstand its ricocheting effects on the international communities. The sudden disappearance of Delano had already sent a lot of ripples among the press, who criticised the government for its insincerity in the handling of the case of the kidnapped U.S. Ambassador, and the sudden disappearance of one of the finest military personnel the NYPD had ever produced.

Public outrage was giving the Secretary of Defense and his Foreign Affairs counterpart unrest. The man at the centre of all the troubles and worries was the Ambassador, who was waging a different kind of war with the Police Forces. An ultimatum of forty-two hours, handed down to the Force to find a solution for both parties to be safe and sound or face sanctions, had been previously allowed to elapse. The current wave of events had unsettled a lot of persons who had vowed to go to any length to bring back a form of neo-colonialism into the framework of the Republic. Senators and House Members were calling the Ambassador's action a bluff. Bills were sponsored by a handful of the house members within the two Chambers of the Federation, which called the government to sever ties with the Americans, on the ground that the American Ambassador had overstepped their boundaries by threatening the sovereignty of a people. The President called for restraint and gave more men to the combined Forces to help in finding the missing US personnel. The time was a quarter past midnight. While the weak were still asleep, it was the ungodly hour for men of the oil and drug world to fraternise. They were on the prowl for big business deals. And Delano had been out of reach for a whole week. All the efforts of the Police Force to track him down, disguised as a team of the Federal government fail. The last time the Force team had been able to get close to him was during his escape with Preye by the sea shore. They had combed all the nooks and crannies of the creeks within their limits, and yet there was no way of finding the man. A fault that was now on the government agencies, who had hurriedly convinced the Federal government to coordinate with the U.S. Department of Defense to aid in the rescue of the kidnapped U.S. Ambassador. When think tanks and gurus in the oil business gathered, top on the agenda was Delano; and the mega oil smuggling, which was about to change their fortunes for the better. But the thought of Delano mixing with the militants could spell doom for them, as the militants had vowed to resist the economic degradation suffered by their people and the land with their last blood. The matter called for urgent attention. So the community of barons met behind closed doors in the halls of one of the most prestigious five star hotels in the capital city of one of the commercial states in the South-South region of the Republic. The room was packed full with top bureaucrats from all walks of life. The Commissioner of Police was also present. He briefed them on the current situation although he was unable to convince them of his exploit with the American special officer, for whom they had been paid so much to keep him out of contact with the militants. The oil barons had no time to waste, since further delay would have serious consequences on the business at hand. The mammoth container ship, The MV Princess, would come in from the Philippines within a few weeks to carry the largest tonnage of crude shipment to Mexico. Mexico was the newly-opened route available to the association of the oil barons of the Republic; a business route that would enable them to exchange black gold for drugs. Drugs were now a new found passion of the political class of the Republic. Almost everybody, from the President down to the last office holder in the polity, had suddenly developed a passion for this white powder that had its origins mostly on the South American continent. The barons had also infiltrated some groups of militants whom they paid heavily to serve as watch dogs along the waterways. These people were not left out either in the drug business, as they helped with the redistribution of small patches on the streets of the region. These few groups of militants were the ones that the spiritual deity had blacklisted. An action the Brotherhood had cashed in on by turning them into rival groups that constantly double-crossed Como's group; the ones that had taken Delano and Preye hostage. They were the criminal groups that had given a bad image to the new struggle, boys who served under the care of the most trusted Police Commissioner in the region, a man who was used by the notorious multinational companies disguising as the Brotherhood. These groups of criminal elements at times stand as Special Force Personnel within the coastal area anytime a hit was planned by the barons. This had made the waterways a death trap, a decoy that worked successfully for the barons in the smuggling business, a group often misrepresented as the Guerrilla unit. The birth of the Guerrilla unit suddenly made a bad run for the barons, who had previously met tremendous success in the oil-smuggling business. The 'Guerrilla Unit' as they liked to be called, broke away from the group of Davis, the investigating police officer assigned to the case of the kidnapped U.S. Ambassador. Davis, over the years, had become the weapon of mass subjugation of other groups within the creeks. The escalation of militant activities within the streets of the South-South came to a standoff and trying to get hold of the new environment overnight made life unbearable for both locals and foreigners. Their actions were not only intended to stop the drug trade, It was also a fight meant to signal an end to the degradation of the region. Before the oil and drug business degenerated into a full-scale war on locals and foreigners, it was a war fought within school campuses. The campus served as a testing ground for the Brotherhood, by initiating the schools' cult members into their fold, with promises of a hitch-free academic session and good grades. An offer most of the unsuspecting lazy students of the various campuses within the South-South states jumped at. They were the ones who had generated street salesmen in the major towns in South-South Nigeria. Running from the 'big heart' down to the 'garden city' and through the ancient city of Calabar, which had become a stronghold of school cult activities, they had helped in spreading drugs on the street. Undergraduates as well as school minors were recruited by the barons through cult activities in institutions. The children who, on leaving school, were not gainfully employed, and whose struggles for any form of livelihood had become a weapon of mass distraction on the business front for the Brotherhood and politicians alike—who enlisted their services in exchange for guns—used the guns for other ventures than the one they were meant for. The high rate of deaths resulting from the activities of this group had led the government to wage an outright, full-scale war on these street renegades. These renegades, in order to escape government punishment, turned the trade war into a political and regional war, a war that immediately gained the support of the local people, who considered the new struggle for the development of the region as a reasonable compensation for the waste, pollution and degradation of the region. The kidnapping of would-be foreign investors became the pretext for demands of billions of Naira from the government. It was in the wake of the government clamp down on these street elements that Davis became a special investigating officer deployed to help clamp down on his former allies in the creeks. This decision generated a lot of controversies and bad blood among his colleagues, some of whom he later enlisted from the street. It was the struggle for the development of the creeks that gave birth to the Guerrilla unit. The Guerrilla unit overnight became the most dreaded pressure group sought after by the barons and government agencies. These little bands of young men under the control of Okitoro, who were loyal to the chosen mouthpiece of the Deity, became the centre of attention, as their activities caused the government and oil smugglers serious nightmare. They made the water ways inaccessible. Their actions caused a lot of worries, especially in the international community, since their activities caused the world economy huge financial downturn in commerce.

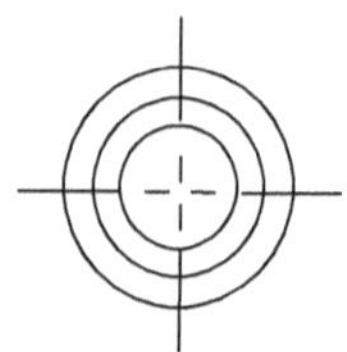

The Escape

Three bodies hung from a rope on a post. They swung to the gentle wave of the wind. Flies hovered around the bodies. The sounds of voices drifted from the camp hut. Three men were sitting around a fire; they gambled with Uno cards, unaware that Okitoro was walking towards their direction. He coughed and they all stood up. Ignoring them, he ordered, "Prepare the Crocodile. Tonight, we must face our destiny. We will fight to rescue the white man."

"Yes, sir," they chorused and Okitoro walked away.

At nine p.m. precisely, in the dead of the night, footsteps ruffled the still and quiet water. The unit men took to the Crocodile that roared to life and glided away in the creek. That evening, Preye was sleeping innocently inside the cell that imprisoned him and Delano. Delano was sitting in the rough mud house with a secured gate made from fine bamboo sticks. Footsteps approached. Delano opened his eyes and tapped Preye. Delano stood up and crouched at one end of the hut. A guard dressed in a black cover walked into view, carrying plates of food on a tray.

Delano made a 'be quiet' sign to Preye, who nodded to the instruction. The guard walked to the cell gate, dropped the tray and fumbled with the heavy padlock holding the door. Opening it, he returned to take the tray of food lying on the ground.

Delano made a quick move on him and in a split second he brought down his heavy fist on the back of his neck. The guard collapsed. Reaching for the lock, Delano flung the door open, and they walked out of the cell. This time Delano took the lead.

Preye followed closely behind finding their way out of the mud hut prison. At the exit, a light shone from the huts that overlooked the cell. Delano scanned for a possible escape route; the only one available to them was a narrow footpath meandering through the hut camp where the guards were playing cards. Counting four shadowy figures reflected by the kerosene light, he crouched on the ground and crept along the footpath, with Preye still closely following behind him. They crept halfway towards the hut, when a figure suddenly appeared through the door. Immediately, they lay on the ground. The guard went behind the hut and they waited for his return. It was now more than five minutes. Delano's instinct told him that it was better for him to outwit the man than wait for the others to come out in search of the guard that had brought them food. At that very thought, Delano instantly glided on the grass and headed to the back of the hut where the guard had disappeared. Preye followed his trail, offering a sign of prayer. In his whole career as a self–acclaimed investigative journalist, never had he encountered death within a hair's breadth as he was right now. Delano crept to the edge of the hut, squatted and walked slowly towards the back of the hut, calculating his every move. Preye managed to crawl to the side of the edge behind Delano and hid himself in a dark spot, taking cover, as he awaited his friend. The guard was leaning over the body of the hut.

Delano picked up a stone and threw it above his head. The stone landed on the other side and drew his attention. As he was turning to face the direction in which the sound had come from, Delano pounced on him and twisted his neck. He placed the unconscious man onto the ground as silently as possible. But the man let out a dying grunt that was overheard by one guard inside the hut.

"Did you hear any sound?"

The others shrugged their shoulders and continued with the game. The guard looked at his companions. Not satisfied, he stood up and walked out of the hut. On discovering one of their men dead on the bare ground, he screamed. The other guards rushed out to meet him. When they saw the dead man, they ran inside the cell hut, only to be greeted by the dead body of the first guard lying on the ground.

Immediately, they ran towards the path leading to the sea bank. Delano dragged Preye along, as he was exhausted from the long trek.

"I can feel the cool breeze. Keep going, we are close."

That was when they heard fast footsteps drawing closer and closer.

"Leave me here, go. I will be fine, just go, they are coming."

The sounds intensified. But even though they became louder, Delano dragged him on. Then they heard the roaring Crocodile coming from the opposite direction.

"I know they will come for you," Preye said weakly. He let go his hand and dropped down on the ground.

"You must come! I need you alive!"

Gunshots flew from behind. Delano ducked. He picked up Preye and carried him, running amidst repeated gunshots. The sound from the Crocodile stopped. Delano ran ahead. The guards got closer, but he ran out of the bush and straight into three fierce-looking men who apprehended him.

Two of them got hold of Delano, and the other one took Preye off him and dragged him away.

Okitoro

The cool, early morning wind blew against Delano, who was tied with his hands above his head to a wooden pole outside. His head was bowed down. Okitoro was dressed in priestly regalia, and he walked out of his room accompanied by three masked guards. One of them was carrying a bucket. They moved towards Delano, who was fast asleep, apparently tired from the escapade of trying to escape. Okitoro and the rest of the guards watched him for a while before speaking.

"Wake him up," he declared in a low but deep voice. Immediately, the guard poured water on him from the bucket. The sharp sting of the cold water woke him up and he writhed in agony.

"Ah. Jeez!" he exclaimed. Raising his head slowly in pain, he looked at them with one eye; the other one was swollen from the blow he received from one of the guards while he protested.

"Good Morning, Delano!" greeted Okitoro.

"Where am I? Who the hell are you? And what do you want from me?" he spat out.

"You almost got yourself killed yesterday," Okitoro replied.

"Fuck you," he shouted back at him. The bucket guard hit him in the stomach. Delano grunted in pain.

Okitoro looked at Delano and commanded the guard, "Untie him and attend to his wound. I will see him when I return from the tour." He signalled to the other two guards to follow him, and the third guard immediately started untying the rope that held Delano to the wooden stick. Okitoro headed off to his daily morning tour of the creek; a tour which gave him the opportunity to get a daily assessment of his constituency. He always devoted at least thirty minutes of his time each day to interact with the locals who were adversely affected by the environmental pollution in the region. He also distributed food items to them, an act that had endeared him and his unit to the heart of the locals, whose support he enjoyed. This routine had come to be a child of necessity, borne out of the protection provided by the people during the formative years of the unit. Delano was tied to a chair in the middle of a spacious room, a basin of water at his feet. A guard walked in with a hand towel and squat before him. He dipped the towel into the water and started massaging the wound with the hot water.

"Arrgh, it hurts!" Delano exclaimed. Getting used to the hot water, he looked at the guard.

"What happened to Preye?" he asked. The guard ignored him and continued with his assignment. There was something weird about this person. Calm, quiet and unwavering. He wondered what he could possibly do to escape. Beaten and broken, he needed to save his energy for a time of possible escape.

"I gotta pee," he shouted out at the guard, who treated him coldly, continuing with the last of the clean-up. Without answering, the man stood up and left the hall. Returning with another bowl, he threw it at him.

"There, pee," the feminine voice hit him. He was amazed, but he pretended not to have noticed.

"My hands, please." The guard looked at him for a moment, and deciding to take a chance. She untied him. Standing on guard, he watched his every move. Delano unzipped his pants, looked at the guard and coughed. The guard hesitated and reluctantly turned to face the wall. Delano picked up the bowl and emptied his bowels into it. Then he coughed again. The guard turned and moved towards the chair, suggesting Delano should sit. Delano walked to the chair but as he was about to sit down, he played a fast one on the guard. He grabbed and twisted the guard's hand behind him and in a split second, Delano pulled off the face mask. His suspicions were right, it wasn't 'him' but 'her'; for the no-nonsense guard was a female. She struggled to free herself from his grip and managed to draw out a knife with one hand.

"Wow, I don't intend any harm!" he protested, raising his hands above his head. There was a bang on the door and he let her walk to the door. Two guards entered the room. Surprised to see her unmasked, they observed the mask lying close to Delano's feet. A second look at Delano's unzipped pants heightened their suspicions. One of the guards then walked towards the female guard and slapped her across the face.

"Shameless whore," he shouted angrily at her in his Ijaw dialect. "Take the American away!" he shouted to the other guard, who immediately took hold of Delano. He struggled hard. Seeing that Delano might overpower the man, the angry-looking guard walked towards them and hit Delano with the butt of his gun. He collapsed.

"Take him away!" he yelled angrily. He then looked at the female guard with disdain, hissed and walked out of the room.

Okitoro sat at the head of a long, bamboo conference table with his trusted men, who had been with him since the inception of the fight against injustice in the region. The Minister, as he was called in the unit, relished the company of his faithful men. The guard who had ordered Delano to be taken away walked into the hall.

"Go, bring the American!" he ordered. One of the guards turned and walked away. He returned with a dirty, scruffy looking Delano.

"What's happened to him?" Okitoro shouted at him. "Where is Amazon?" he demanded. The atmosphere became tense. Everyone gazed at the messy Delano.

"Danga, bring her here!" Okitoro ordered. Danga hesitated.

"Did you hear what I just said?" shouted Okitoro. Danga left and returned with Amazon, who herself was in a more battered state than Delano. On seeing her, Okitoro was perplexed.

"Tamara! (God) Who did this to you?" he exclaimed.

Her eyes darted to Danga. Okitoro's face contorted in a grimace.

"Your obsession for…for…her…I told you, will cause your death, if you don't control yourself," Okitoro stammered in rage. He continued to snarl at Danga.

"Lock him up!"

Two of the seated members of the unit got up, and lay hold of Danga dragging him off.

"Go, clean yourself up," Okitoro told Amazon. He looked at Delano, and fear gripped him.

"And you too American." Delano left in company of Amazon.

"The meeting will be held later. For now, I have other things to attend to."

Okitoro got up and left, pulling along with him the beautiful robe he was wearing. They all followed in his step, feeling despair.

The commissioner was awoken by his cell phone the very night Delano had escaped from the grip of the militants who had abducted him. He left quickly for the office. Pacing up and down, he wondered what the hell had happened to the American. For years, he served the government and the oil barons faithfully.

Why was this happening now? When just a few months separated him from his retirement and into a peaceful life? Before the recent events, he had promised his wife a trip to the Bahamas, where he planned to buy a home for them to live after retirement.

He savoured the last of his successful deals with the oil barons, especially the one concerning the mega container ship, the MV Princess. His share of the loot would run into several millions of dollars. Now he sat and saw all that going down the drain. The phone calls from the high and mighty in the corridors of power were weighing down seriously on him too. While lost in thought, Davis walked into the office, unannounced.

"Get out of here!" thundered the chief. Davis turned to leave the office.

"Come back here, fool! What have you found out?" the commissioner lashed out. Davis with his head bowed, "Nothing much, sir." Davis replied in a shaky voice.

The commissioner's gaze swept over him in anger. Davis knew the man hated incompetence, and he hadn't been giving the assignment his best shot or so it seemed.

"Sir, the boys are combing all the nooks for possible clues." he added.

"Combing is not enough, Davis. I want results! It is either Delano, or Okitoro, or we all go down!" shouted the Chief.

"We are doing our best, sir," Davis managed to say.

"Yeah, I know that."

The commissioner paused and then looked at him intensely with disgust.

"Your best is not good enough. We paid you to deliver results, not a try. So get out of here, and bring me results!"

At that moment, the office phone rang. The commissioner stared at it with sunken eyes, filled with fear, fear of another threat from the pipers who had long played the tune he danced to! He stood there, motionless. Davis watched him. He knew the man for years, but he had never seen him in this state of mayhem. The commissioner at last mustered enough courage and picked up the phone.

"Hello?" he spoke with an astonishingly calm voice.

"What?" he shouted, drawing the attention of Davis.

"Ok, am on my way!" He hung up and grabbed his car keys from the table, and rushed out of the office.

"You come with me!" the commissioner yelled at Davis, and Davis ran along with him.

Sitting in his office, Okitoro took his cell phone and searched for a number and dialled it.

"Bring him in," he ordered.

"Ok sir." The line went dead. The door of the office opened. A guard came in with Delano. Okitoro beckoned to a seat.

"Leave us," he ordered, and the guard left.

"Sit down, my friend." Delano gazed at him. Okitoro nodded to him.

"I'm not your enemy. You need me to succeed, and I need you to help my people survive." He pointed to one of the vacant chairs again. Delano drew out one, and sat down, watching him closely.

"Thank you for obliging me. Sorry for my men's behaviour, but he could not help it with Amazon. I brought them all here after their village was destroyed, and their parents were killed, and since then Danga has had this insufferable passion for her ever since I picked them from that rubble."

Delano's gazed narrowed.

"You are wondering why I speak so well, unlike the others." He smiled, as Delano kept his gaze at him. Okitoro opened one of the office drawers, brought out an envelope and sent it spinning on the table towards him. Delano picked it up and opened it. He pulled out a university degree certificate with the bold logo of Stanford University.

Delano read the paper, and saw that Okitoro had obtained honours in International Relations. Okitoro's expression was blank.

"So why are you doing this?" asked Delano.

"My people called me." He paused then continued., "And I yielded to their cry."

"But there are other things you could have done with this!" insisted Delano.

"Why are you here, my friend?" Okitoro asked him.

"To rescue the kidnapped U.S. Ambassador."

"And why is that?" Okitoro inquired.

"There is an American citizen who needs the help of his country, to regain his freedom, and it is an honour and responsibility given to me to carry out that assignment successfully. I must deliver. There is no stopping me."

Okitoro looked him in the eyes and let out a mild laugh. Delano did not wince.

"It is also my responsibility to deliver my people from the oppression of degradation and environmental shackles from oppressive governmental agencies." He paused and thought for a split second.

"They have brought unimaginable hardships on my people, and that is what we are fighting against."

He stood up and walked up to Delano. Delano watched the massive, broad shouldered man walk towards him.

"What about the U.S. Ambassador?" he asked Okitoro.

"If I had the U.S. Ambassador, I wouldn't be here with you. It is a ruse by the government and its agencies to smear our activities, my people and the oil rich region of the Niger Delta which is controlled by greedy and callous multinational companies supported by some criminal militant elements sponsored by these multinationals. Those are the ones who portray our activities in a bad light to the international community."

"And how does that concern the kidnapped U.S. Ambassador?" Delano questioned.

"The biggest shipment of crude oil will be done in the next few weeks, as has always been the case with all these multinationals which have carried out the exploitation of oil in the region for decades, without ever considering the plight and welfare of the locals. As we speak, a vessel is coming in from Mexico."

So?" Delano inquired.

"They are trying to keep us off the waterways by hanging the kidnapping on our activities, so we won't be able to ward off this illegal business that is about to take place, because the government will be on us, thinking that we have the U.S. Ambassador, just as they made you believe it."

Becoming emotional, he continued, "This, we must stop, as we have vowed to do until the government responds to our demands on the Memorandum of Understanding, the declaration we made available to them and other agencies and non-governmental organisations, and the request also made by our leaders after the death of Wiwa, who was brutally murdered by the military junta of the now late dictator, General Sani Abacha, for standing and speaking up against the deplorable state of our land. They are not only stealing our black gold. They have filled the streets with drugs. The youths are becoming their target."

Delano started to feel some empathy. "So as for the U.S. Ambassador, who now has him?" Okitoro fell silent at his question. Delano looked at him intently and wondered what was going through his mind.

"We will help you find the U.S. Ambassador."

Delano's eyes popped wide open.

"We will, but on one condition, and according to our terms." What could that be? Delano became really interested.

"Make our demands known to the international community. They must know that we are a just and peaceful people, who are only fighting for the development of our region, and for the resources that have been stolen from the environment and pursue all pending cases and awarded compensation made to the development of our land paid. Only on this condition will we work together."

Delano, absorbed in his thoughts, watched the serious-looking Okitoro.

"Ok, where do we begin?" Okitoro's face broke into a wide grin. He walked over to the intercom on his table and pressed the button, Buzz. The door swung open.

A guard came in carrying a document, and handed it to him. Then, he left silently. Okitoro stared at the document. He picked it up and dusted it, and then handed it over to Delano.

"These are our demands, most of which we have submitted to successive governments." Delano took the document and read the front cover. Okitoro pressed the button again. Buzz.

The door opened and another guard walked in.

"The Crocodile is ready, sir."

"Thank you, Spoonface," Okitoro replied and the guard left.

"They are waiting for us." He smiled at Delano.

"Who are they?" asked Delano.

"Not so fast, there is still time to meet them."

Okitoro walked out of the large room, with Delano following closely behind.

Inspector Davis sat in the lobby of the trauma ward of the general hospital, agitated. He looked at his watch and frowned. Time had flown past him without his awareness. The commissioner came out with a doctor. Davis saw them and rose to his feet.

"How is her condition, sir?" he asked feverishly.

"I promise you sir, we will do our best. She will be fine, but like I said earlier, she will need a specialist to monitor her case very closely," the doctor answered. Dotun's wife had just had another severe seizure of the lower spine as a result of her health condition.

"I will see to that, my dear friend, but for now, do all you can. My confidence in you over the years has not waned," the commissioner replied in an unsteady voice. The doctor put a reassuring arm on his shoulder.

"Go home. Tomorrow, when you come, you will see her in a much better state, but like I have advised, please, consider it seriously."

"I will, I will." He looked up at this most trusted man. But every day things were becoming more difficult for him. He now cursed all the time, asking rhetorical questions. The sour feeling caused by the recent strain could be seen on his face.

Davis urged him on as they walked out of the hospital. Driving, the commissioner back to the office, the commissioner gave Davis some details about future events.

"Son, I will be out of circulation for a while. My wife needs attention." The police radio interrupted him.

"Alpha, alpha, the American was spotted by the joint team on board a Crocodile with militants on the Oporozar river, destination unknown. Our surveillance team is closely monitoring them."

Picking up the radio, Davis caught the voice and cut into the conversation.

"All routes on the alert! All naval boats on guard! I'm on my way."

"Copy, sir. Over and out." Davis looked at the commissioner.

"Drop me at the station, and do what you have got to do," the commissioner said wearily.

"Yes…sir" Davis replied as he hit on the gas pedal.

"Davis?" the commissioner called gently.

"Yes, sir?" he responded.

"Don't worry, go…go!"

Davis noticed the way he repeated the words in a voice laden with emotion. Concentrating on driving, his heart went out to the commissioner. Davis just couldn't imagine the torment commissioner must have gone through since the kidnapping of the U.S. Ambassador. Guilt flooded his mind and his thoughts ran in uncontrollable frenzy. He cried out in pain.

"Okitoro."

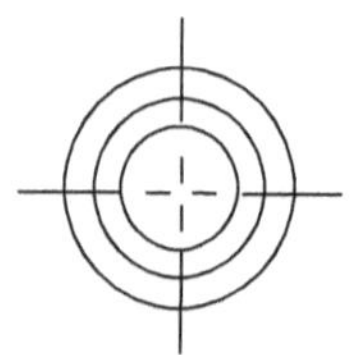

The Creeks

The heavy thud of feet could be heard in the dense undergrowth. Delano in the company of friends emerged from the bush to a pool of water mixed with oil.

"This spill occurred two weeks ago. This is the only source of water that runs through the villages around here, and as you can see aquatic life is being destroyed."

Okitoro addressed him as he bent down and scooped water from the river with his hands. Delano and the other members of Okitoro's unit numbering over fifteen watched him. They walked on the carpet of grass which, despite suffering from the effects of the spill, still adorned the beautiful landscape gracefully. They reached a hectare of farmland overgrown with cassava plants. The coarse leaves of the farm products looked pitiful.

"Jeez! What happened here?"

"This happens every season," Okitoro commented. Delano wore an expressionless face.

"These plants are just weeks from being harvested," Okitoro continued.

"The main source of water supply has been contaminated by oil spills that leaked from one of the old pipelines traversing most of our land. When this happened, we wrote to the joint ventures, but for over a year now, nothing has been done, not even an assessment term from either the government or the companies. They have never bothered to come and look at the extent of the damage the spill has caused."

Delano was moved to tears.

His host continued, "Except for Amnesty International and the Campaign for Democracy and Human Rights Defence, among the very few non-governmental organisations, who have written various reports, articles and recommendations, calling on the government to evacuate the locals from the villages, as they have been dying in large numbers due to a strange disease that the United Nations Environmental Protection Agencies (UNEPA) have discovered." Okitoro turned round abruptly.

"Let's leave for the village now."

The amphibious combat craft known as The Crocodile was anchored on the head bridge at Gbaramatu waterside. The harsh smell of death hovered in the atmosphere and it meant squalor and poverty for the surrounding villages. The activities of haphazard oil spills and illegal oil bunkers caused environmental pollution. To make matters worse, the oil barons who enjoy the benefits from these atrocities finance the perpetrators. The villagers were going about their daily routine of scooping up dead fish, which served as their means of survival. The harsh realities of their lands' destruction made it difficult for the locals to get enough foodstuff for their daily consumption. This had brought untold hardships. They came out in numbers to welcome their unsung hero. Crowds surrounded Okitoro and Delano, while the guards were watching attentively. The convoy moved along the dusty, unpaved road that was begging for the government's attention. The crowd escorted them. To some of the villagers, the occasion was one of nostalgia. These people had not come across an American for a long time. Delano followed Okitoro. He noticed a big house ahead of them. The villagers tried to get his attention, and some of them, especially the children, took hold of his hand. He laughed with them, and walked on. When they got close to the house, the crowd formed a circle outside, to Delano's wonderment as he looked on thoughtfully.

"This way please," Okitoro pointed to the way leading to the palace, made from fine bamboo, trash and material from the mangrove forest. Delano looked around cautiously. The excited crowd urged him in, so he followed Okitoro. The other militants mounted guard outside the palace. The atmosphere over Gbaramatu village was disturbing. Birds chirped. An eagle hovered in mid-air but the mood of celebration over the palace became tense. An uneasy wind refused to dance to the sweet tunes the palm trees naturally played. The plantain trees and all the other trees, which adorned the village, ceased their dance. His Royal Highness, the Pere of the Egbema kingdom, joined them. Okitoro stood up and introduced Delano in his native language. His Royal Highness acknowledged him and greeted him, also addressing him in the native dialect through Okitoro. His Royal Highness expressed displeasure about the deplorable state of the land.

"But as much as I hate what is happening to my people, I must state that, as a member of the older generation, I warn you, younger ones, to be restrained in the mood and manner that this course is taking, because…"

Okitoro immediately cut him off, already sensing the direction in which his speech was heading. To him, this was cowardice, withdrawal from the course by the same man, he and his men had constantly protected and provided for. The Pere of the Egbema kingdom was engaging in an argument about why he was withdrawing his support from them despite having support from a powerful American when suddenly, screams came from the crowd outside. Sporadic gunfire followed by heavy shelling. The crowd of villagers dispersed in different directions; the guards outside exchanged fire with members of the Joint Military Force. Okitoro and Delano rushed out, but could not advance, as the men of the Force were closer than they expected. Okitoro handed Delano a rifle and looked at him. The look in his eyes spoke volumes, and Delano immediately understood that it was action time. As much as Delano hated to be drawn into the feud, he remembered that the only way he could get to the U.S. Ambassador and escape these firefights was to help them out. Delano took the rifle from Okitoro. They joined in the fire fight, forcing the Joint Force to retreat.

While retreating, the Joint Force had to call for backup. The bullets engulfed the entire village, immediately turning it into a ghost town. The civilians deserted the whole place. Suddenly, a gunman came from the opposite direction. A few meters away from Okitoro, the man aimed his gun at him. He was going to pull the trigger, when Delano shot him down. Okitoro, hearing the shot, turned around, surprised. He nodded his appreciation to Delano. Okitoro realised that he had lost a lot of men. And he decided to retreat. He whistled to Delano and waved him over. They ran through the palace and, jumping into the thick bush and quickly disappeared into the dense vegetation. Okitoro and Delano with a handful of survivors wandered in the tropical forest, surrounded by water. They meandered their way through the forest as anticipation clouded their reason. Delano watched Okitoro closely and saw the fear in the celebrated leader of the small Guerrilla unit. He wondered what was happening to the man who seemed fearless, immovable and strong.

"Where are we?" Delano asked, straight-faced as they entered the creek. Pressing their way through, Okitoro ordered the others in his native dialect. "Move! Move! and get the Crocodile! They're coming!"

Delano noticed them running through the water. He looked back, saw nothing, and struggled to accelerate through the resistance caused by the water. The Passport 90, a military speed boat ideal for creeks and rivers appeared from the opposite direction. They watched the PT-90, the infamous Crocodile gliding into view with light machine guns mounted on the port and starboard sides. Okitoro saw Spoonface, who had stayed back at the fort. He stood up and waved to them. The Crocodile increased its speed towards them. They jumped into it, and the Crocodile sped off. The Crocodile approached the fort. Cold air engulfed the boat. The whole place looked deserted. Getting out of the boat, they saw dead bodies scattered on the ground. Among them was Danga, and there lay Amazon, badly injured. Gasping for breath, Okitoro rushed over to her, the others joined him, she was nearly dead.

"They… were… here," she struggled for words.

"Who were they?" he asked as his eyes glistened with unshed tears. She opened her right palm to reveal the barons' emblem. Delano walked close to her and took a look at the emblem. His mind flashed back to the picture at the commissioner's office, the tattoo on the dead woman's shoulder. Amazon was gasping for breath.

"My God, hang on!" Okitoro cried. He carried her, and they walked into the hall of the hut.

Delano pulled off his shirt, revealing his bare, hairy body. He fell on the small bed of the room within the camp. Lying on his back he gazed at the ceiling. Through a tiny hole, a ray of light pierced the thatched roof, and Delano pondered over the events of the last few days. Since his escape from the camp, he had been hosted by a band of militants and shot at by heavily armed foes. The smiling face of the young woman at the club now invaded his thoughts. Delano recalled the innocent young woman's cry, "They want to kill me!"

Then, Okitoro's passionate plea, "In this document is all we are asking for… you take it to the world. We will help you rescue the U.S. Ambassador."

These words echoed in his head. The memories of the violent explosion of guns at the village coincided with a heavy bang on the door that woke him up from his trance. Delano waited for a second. There was another bang again. He tiptoed to the door and strained his left eye to peep through one of the holes of the heavily-built door. When Delano saw it was Spoonface, he opened the door.

"Boss wants to see you," Spoonface said.

Delano looked at his wristwatch. It read fifteen minutes past ten p.m. He shot him an uncertain glance for a moment and then stepped back into the room. Returning with his shirt, he walked away with Spoonface.

The door of the hall swung open. Delano walked in to meet Okitoro, who sat with his back facing the entrance. Okitoro swirled around. The expression on his face told Delano that all was not well. He took a seat close to him.

"We are leaving this camp. The government troops are closing in on us," Okitoro shouted out.

"So what happens to the U.S. Ambassador?" asked Delano, ignoring his remark.

"Spoonface and Shaka will get you to the border to meet our brothers. My men will fill you in on the details." At that statement, Okitoro got up and hurriedly left the room.

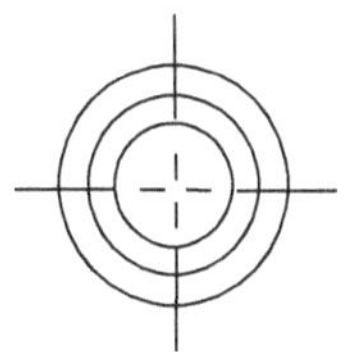

A Better Glimpse

The stars engulfed the night sky. They inched their way into the night stealthily, occasionally interrupted by sporadic croaking of amphibious creatures. A heavy splash in the water indicated that they had company. Reflections shimmered on the surface of the water. Patiently, they waited and watched, but curiosity overrode prudence. As the moonlight fell on the water revealing their watery path, the reflection of a multi-coloured beast gliding through the water had them retreating. The animal stopped. Spoonface raised his rifle silently and aimed at it. Everything around them came to a standstill. Heart beats quickened and veins pumped adrenalin furiously. The sudden rising of the python from the water sent them reeling dangerously over the edge. Spoonface and Shaka, engaged their weapons and aimed at the beast. But Delano hushed them with a wave of his hand, silently ordering them to lower their guns.

The snake was on their heels. They were petrified. The python seemed to scan the whole area meticulously looking for prey. Then all of a sudden, it turned back and glided away. The men were rooted to the spot, unable to move. Gradually, the tension eased up, and finally they heaved a huge sigh of relief as they realised the python had retreated into its dense mangrove habitat, and they had narrowly escaped being killed. They continued on their journey. Another splash made them come to an abrupt halt again. Caution shrouded them as they listened carefully. They could detect voices from people walking through the water. Delano, in the company of Spoonface and Shaka, trod carefully in the quiet night, heavily armed. All of a sudden, a flash of light fell on them from the distance.

"We are close," Spoonface said in a frightened voice. They walked into a band of fierce-looking, armed men, who on seeing them turned around. Spoonface beckoned to Delano to follow closely. The band of armed men walked towards the thatched house, along with Spoonface, Shaka and Delano. Delano scanned the surrounding area. The calmness and peace he felt about the environment, reassured him. He could trust Okitoro, but still didn't know the details and had yet to find out. They went into the house. The interior revealed a modern, lavishly-furnished home. To his surprise, Shaka, the leader of the group, spoke to Spoonface in a native tongue. Delano guessed it was an order, for they left immediately.

"Please, make yourself at home," Spoonface told Delano. "He will send for us later" Before he finished talking, Shaka threw himself on one of the chairs. Delano cautiously took to another chair. The three men fell asleep in no time, due to exhaustion from their rigorous journey.

After being hurriedly sent to Como, Delano had a series of nightmares. He saw the dead woman with the tattoo on her shoulder, telling him how they wanted him dead. He was confronted by the scene of Preye bleeding to death, as well as the sporadic gunfire that flattened the village to the ground, and killed dozens of hospitable children he met in the company of Okitoro. He twisted in the chair painfully, trying to make himself comfortable on the couch, but the scenario which had taken the lives of his beloved wife and son played before him.

He saw himself standing helpless, unable to help them; he ran and then found himself in the Middle East, watching rebel forces killing innocent children and women. A seven-year-old girl cried out and called to him for help. As he was trying to reach out to the child, a bullet from one of the gunmen caught her in the heart and she died. Delano screamed violently and woke up. Gasping and panting for breath, he looked around and saw Spoonface and Shaka snoring quietly. He turned in the direction of the large wall clock as it chimed on the midnight hour. A moment later, Delano noticed a slight push to the door. Two armed men walked in, and were startled to find him awake. They became cautious, expecting him to do something funny. But Delano just looked at them warily without moving. One of the two men tapped Spoonface and Shaka on the shoulder, and they woke up.

"Come with us," one of them ordered. They turned round and left. Spoonface led the men, who all walked into the deep dark night.

The room was dimly lit. Light pierced through the ceiling from the moon that hung outside. The cool air sang filling the room. A match stick was struck, producing a tiny flame from the hurricane lamp on the table. The light from the lamp revealed Como, dressed in a black outfit and holding a shotgun. He sat on the only chair in the room. The door swung open, and the guards walked in, closely followed by the emissaries and their American companion.

"Leave us," Como's voice issued forth. The guards left immediately. He threw an envelope onto the floor, and gestured with his head towards Delano.

"Pick it up," he ordered. Delano bent down cautiously and picked it up.

Como continued, "It belongs to you, I suppose?"

"Where the hell did you get this?" Delano barked.

"That is never the way to keep a promise. Okitoro ordered it to be given to you, before…" Como stopped and bowed his head.

"Before what?" Delano inquired. "What has happened to him?"

Spoonface and Shaka threw questioning looks in Como's direction.

"He was captured the night you people left the camp. The parcel was delivered to me this morning at the training camp by one of his men."

"How can I get to the city?" Delano blurted out, "I need to get to the city and finish my business!"

"Not so fast, my dear American."

"But I have to! The U.S. Ambassador must be found."

"Yes, you are right," replied Como, "But where can you find him?"

Delano inhaled deeply.

"Okitoro said the answer lies with you. So what do you know?"

Como exhaled gently.

"I don't know much. But I am going to tell you the little I know. Not that it matters, but because it will vindicate us in the international eye, for we are not just a group of people who are fighting the government by causing chaos, we are a group of citizens who are demanding a better living environment; good roads, schools, health and shelter from the resources that are produced from our own soil. It has greatly enriched both the high and the mighty in today's world, including your country, America. And yet we die in abject neglect and poverty," Como said.

Recalling the incident that had taken place on the day the U.S. Ambassador was kidnapped, Como continued, "I was assigned by the Spiritual Deity as the leader for the freedom of my people to spearhead the rescue of the U.S. Ambassador. Our intel reliably informed us he would be kidnapped on his way to the commission site. While I was hiding in the bush with my men assigned for the mission, the convoy came along. We were preparing to move in, when an old vehicle came along, only to break down in the middle of the road. The agents attached to the convoy tried to move the vehicle off the road. Right then, we heard sporadic gunshots shelling everyone to pieces. As I watched, I see this guy outfitted in camouflage wear and with superior firepower. It was then I knew we had been double-crossed, so I had to move my men off the scene."

Como dipped his hand into the breast pocket of the black jacket he was wearing on top of his uniform, and brought out an emblem, which he threw on the floor. Delano bent down again and picked the emblem up. To his greatest surprise, it had the same drop-of-oil symbol on the emblem.

"I have seen this before," he said, almost inaudibly.

"Yes, you have. Immediately they noticed you were getting curious, the very moment you stepped into the case of the kidnapping, they had you framed by setting the young woman on you."

"What!?" Delano exclaimed.

"Yes, though she was not supposed to die. But when you insisted on seeing her after your bail, it meant doom for the barons," replied

Como.

"And why was that?" asked Delano.

Como took a deep breath, exhaled and continued.

"Because right from the club, the very night you went drinking with Davis, they sensed you were attracted to her, and so they had to kill her."

Delano breathed heavily. "But that was too much!"

"No, it was not too much…," Como cut him off. "She knew too much, and you getting close to her brought doom."

"Knew too much?" inquired Delano. "Wait a minute—" the light went off in Delano's head.

"Yes?" replied Como.

"She has been working undercover for the unit since she was twelve years old, the price her father paid for an unfulfilled promise to the oil barons. The failed business deals involved misappropriation of tax payers' money…"

Wait! Are you saying she is one of your men?" Delano exclaimed.

"Yes, she is."

"So how then are the militants…I mean your group, linked to all this?" Delano inquired.

"In the next few weeks, a shipment will be coming from Mexico."

"Shipment of arms?" asked Delano.

"No, they have now found a new trade, since the international treaties on free arms and nuclear weapons restrictions are being imposed. They have now gone into the counterfeit and designer drug business. They will bring shipments from Colombia, India, Mexico and the far East; a trade route the present administration has been trying to close for years through drug enforcement agencies. The kidnapping of the U.S. Ambassador is a detour."

"A detour!?" Delano exploded.

"Yes, like I said, a shipment is coming from Mexico in a few weeks, and the kidnapping of the U.S. Ambassador is meant to place the Federal troops on our trail, making the waterways free for the easy passage of their dirty business deals which they usually exchange for millions of barrels of oil."

A deadly silence cloaked the small room. The revelation also surprised Spoonface and Shaka, who over the years, considered the oil fight a tribal vendetta. With the present information they just heard, they became remorseful. Their real motive for joining the fight was just beginning to stare them in the face. Their initial decision of making millions of Nigerian Dollars through the struggle now appeared selfish. Their weedy desires intolerant.

"These barons, where can they be found?" Delano spoke again, breaking the silence in the room.

"The only man who has that answer is Davis."

"Davis?" Delano exclaimed in utter surprise.

"Yes Davis. Like in other parts of the world, these men are not really what they seem. He was one of those who started this mission. He sold out on the Guerrilla unit for a plate of porridge in the wake of the government's offer of amnesty; the final straw set in motion, to break our backs in our fight for our rights. We have no other option now than to accept the amnesty the Nigerian Federal government is offering us. That, again, the barons do not want."

"And why is that?" Delano asked.

"The waterways will become free of militant activities and no longer serve as bait for mercenaries to carry out the oil barons' dirty deeds. The Federal troops will easily close in on them. As for Davis, he holds the key to the U.S. Ambassador's whereabouts. We don't want to get further involved in the issue of the U.S. Ambassador, so at dawn, my men will lead you to the city," Como replied.

Como stood up. "Get some sleep. The night is far spent."

As he walked past them, heading for the exit, Delano called out to him.

"Wait, where can I find Davis?"

Como ignored the question but answered, "Go, and take a rest. It's very late already."

Delano then opened the door and stepped out into the night, with the guard leading the way.

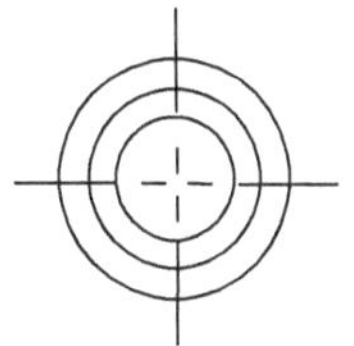

The Encounter

Delano walked into the entrance hall of the Grand Hotel, one of the most expensive of its kind, owned by a renowned businessman of Delta-Ibo extraction. He went straight to the bar, drew one of the neatly arranged stools from under the table, and sat down. He ordered a glass of squash. The barman poured some of the liquid from the bottle he picked from the bar rack and passed it to him. Delano slid some Naira bills to him. The barman picked up the notes, and flipping through them, immediately noticed the emblem with the drop of oil. Delano looked at him and noticed his expression change. He took a quick sweep of the entire hall, waiting for the man's next move.

"I don't come cheap," he heard the barman say. Noticing that the barman was game, Delano cleared his throat. "I pay for what I have."

The barman turned away.

"What is your price?" Delano inquired. A customer entered the bar. They exchanged pleasantries, and the man ordered cans of Heineken. He paid for them and left the bar. Delano brought out five two-hundred-Dollar bills and placed them on the table. The barman looked at him as he was sipping his drink.

"Penthouse, Hotel de la Baroness," the barman said, returning to his job of cleaning the glasses. Delano gulped the rest of his squash, stood up and left immediately. The barman watched him walk through the sliding door. He picked up the intercom from the drinks shelf and dialled a number. Delano sped through 5th Avenue. The metallic-coloured Camry breezed along the road with much precision, like a Boeing 747. Turning off the highway into the by-pass to the station on the Government Reserve Area expressway, he observed an SUV in his rear mirror. He watched it for a moment. Convinced it was definitely on his trail, he brought out his GPS road map and quickly checked for an exit on his route.

Holding on to the steering wheel, he discovered that there was a T-split junction ahead of him. He pressed the pedal, accelerating up to 70 miles per hour. As he sped on, he looked into his rear-view mirror. The car was gone.

Sensing no further danger, he eased off the pedal. But looking ahead again, he saw the SUV coming at him from the opposite direction. He had no time to divert from the car. He pressed the brakes attempting to avert them, but he collided with a tree. Four fierce-looking, masked men came out of and went over to the visibly unconscious Delano on the wheel. Pulling him out, they carried him into the SUV and drove away.

The hasty footsteps of someone could be heard approaching the door of the small holding cell. When he opened the door, rays of sunlight lit up the interior. The man walked in. He ran his hand on the surface of the wall, looking for the light switch. When he pressed it, a tiny green light came on from a bulb that hung in a corner of the holding cell.

"Who is there?" asked Delano, who had been tied, a bag made of sackcloth over his head. Someone walked over to him and pulled off the bag covering his head. Delano squeezed his eyes as the light fell on him. Gradually opening them, he looked at the figure before him.

"Davis!" he called out.

"You are the most foolish American I have ever come across in my entire time in this business!" Davis cried out.

"Business…What business?" Delano asked, surprised.

"I am here to offer you a deal. You take it, the U.S. Ambassador lives. You refuse the Ambassador dies. And the blame will be on your conscience, as well as your wife's and child's." Delano's eyes revealed his surprise. How did he know?

"Don't be surprised Delano. What you are into is far beyond your comprehension, and you are insignificant in the grand scheme of it all," Davis replied

"And what plan is that?" Delano cut in.

Davis stared at him for a few seconds.

"Don't play the wise-ass detective Delano. Right from the moment I set my eyes on you, you struck a chord in my mind. If you want to know, you are one of the few men who have been sent on a mission like this one, and has survived it. Do you know why?"

Delano looked at him with eyes wide open.

"It is because your government and top government officers are involved in this. Have you ever wondered why nobody before has asked questions about the activities going on with the oil and its people?"

Delano continued to gaze at him, listening with rapt attention.

"Billions of dollars from our business have kept the people mighty, both in high and low positions…" he paused, the continued, "So like I said, the choice is yours." He turned pretending to leave.

"And what exactly are these options?" Delano inquired.

"Walk away and the U.S. Ambassador will be given to you in forty-eight hours. And half a million dollars will be made available to any bank of your choice, anywhere in the world."

The deadline given by Davis corresponded with the time when the Mexican vessel was expected. Enough time for the deal to be concluded, a battle the militants were fighting hard to prevent. The militants in the riverine area would fight to stop the continual degradation of the people and their horrible conditions, even if it meant using their last drop of blood. Delano feared that he might not be able to rescue the U.S. Ambassador, and more so fail to fulfil the promise he made to Okitoro.

The deal looked good; half a million US Dollars and the U.S. Ambassador walking away untouched. He was caught in between. The money sounded reasonable. A life in Acapulco was what he dreamt of, and owning a home on the Mexican beach appealed to his senses—a dream he had been working to achieve; a promise he made to Janice during their courtship. Realising this dream and giving that place the name of his beloved wife, Janice, would make her rest in perfect peace. But lives lay in the balance, the lives of innocent children and women. And of course, any compromise could jeopardise the image of the American government. These thoughts were echoing through his mind, when suddenly Davis interrupted him.

"This offer could not only make Janice rest in peace. It would also allow you to live the kind of life you have always dreamt of in Acapulco."

"Woo, stop right there! How come you know all these things about me, when we barely know each other?" Delano interrogated.

"In the choice of your refusal to accept this offer made to you now by the Brotherhood, I am afraid, my friend…"

Davis turned and walked away from the holding cell, closing the door behind him. Delano called him back. Davis re-entered the room.

"So this is the price for impoverishing your own people, killing and damaging them?" Delano looked hard at him.

Davis' eyes widened in surprise. Then his gaze narrowed dangerously, looking intently at Delano. Delano's gaze was still hard, silently probing his unscrupulous double life. Davis planted a tight, closed fist on Delano's chest. Delano fell to the ground and groaned in pain.

"Don't you ever talk to me like that again!" He stormed out of the holding cell, swearing under his breath. His face was an angry mask as he sat down in his office. He suddenly got up, and paced his small office. For a moment there, he reflected on Delano's question. The past few years, since he started to work for the barons against the rural populace, no spoken word had penetrated the seat of his conscience, so deeply. He had spearheaded the blowing up of the Atlas Cove that had caused a huge loss of money to the government. He had also facilitated the killing of prominent activists who stood against the oil barons in their quest for power, political dominance and control of the Niger Delta. Confused and agitated, Davis picked up a file lying on his table and left his office. He drove through the lonely Minister Avenue, heading towards the Hotel de la Baroness. Delano's question kept running through his mind. He suddenly put the car in reverse, and headed back home. Davis knew that Delano cared about absolutely nothing after losing his wife and son to a car accident. He inserted his key in the keyhole of his door and flung it open. He walked in, throwing the bunch of keys on the table, as he did, and then made his way to the kitchen, and opened the refrigerator. He pulled out a cold bottle of beer, popped it open and gulped down half of the contents. He exhaled heavily, and went back into the sitting room, and threw himself on the couch.

A black CRV drove through the lonely avenue, heading towards the Hotel de Baroness. It stopped at the large steel gate and honked its horn several times. The steel gate slid open; the black CRV drove inside and the steel gate automatically closed up. Davis stepped out of the car.

After locking it, he turned round and saw gunmen coming out from all corners of the building. They headed towards him. He screamed and he woke up jumping up from the couch.

"Jeez!" he yelled. "It was a dream," he muttered, exhaling in relief.

Wiping the beads of sweat trickling down his face, he picked up his drink and continued from where he left off, taking a huge sip from the bottle. Davis rested his head back on the couch and let his mind wonder about the dream he just had. He wasn't a man known to be easily scared or moved by anything. But since his encounter with Delano in the holding cell earlier on, his conscience had been shaken badly by his words. This wasn't because Davis had not heard those words before, but for a total stranger to express such concern for the people he hardly knew reflected a strong and uncompromising character trait. Tears slid down his face as he felt beaten to the bone. In a calculated move, Davis stood up, picked up his shirt and walked out of the apartment with a heavy heart, and thinking to himself that this Delano was the shining example of what an American with the license to carry a gun could do when motivated.

The Shake-Up

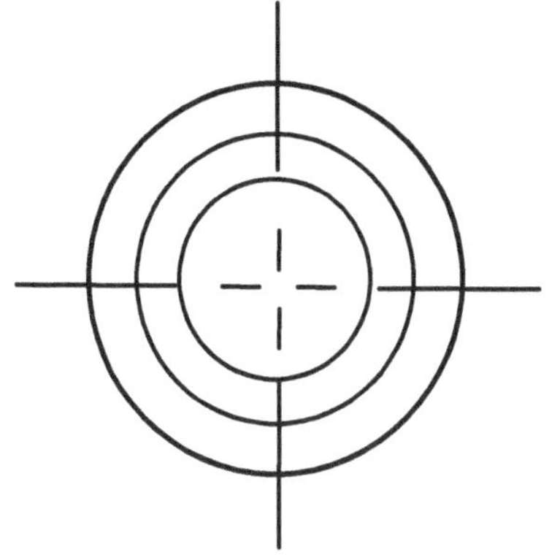

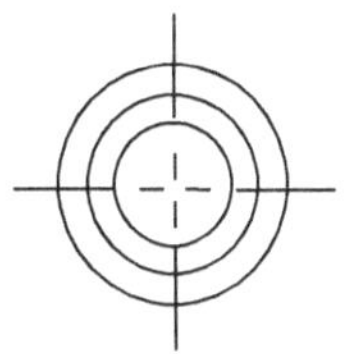

A Premonition

The Commissioner of Police was still in the office at 10 p.m. Anxiety and worry were written all over him, as he dialled a number on the intercom. He placed the receiver on his ear and waited for an answer. He heard the tone ringing as he waited in anticipation for the voice at the other end. But the tone suddenly went dead. He banged the receiver on the set, and in anger made to bring out his cell phone from the neatly ironed Ben Shaman white shirt he was putting on. As he was reaching for it, He noticed a stain on the shirt and his anxiety grew. Although he refused to believe it, it had become something which turned out to be true in all cases, that whenever he saw a stain on his clothes, there was bound to be trouble ahead. Stains were related to problems as far as he was concerned. So, he endeavoured as much as possible to avoid stains, no matter how small they were. The last time he had one on his shirt, was when his wife had been diagnosed with her illness. And that was the very first time he started attaching importance to the superstition. Another instance, was when he lost his darling mother, on that fateful day in January 1979. His mother had come over to tend to his nursing wife who had just given birth to their first child. He left them both happy and hearty that morning as he left for the office. While he was on his way, his Peugeot 404 developed a leak in the oil hose. He was trying to fix the problem, when the oil splashed on him.

He became so gloomy he did not understand what was going on. An hour later, he was called by one of his colleagues at the Police Force headquarters to take a call. It was on the phone that he heard the wailing voice of his wife breaking the news of his mother's death to him. Yet she had looked well that morning. Nobody knew what had gone wrong. So since the illness of his wife, which he also blamed on the stain on his shirt, Adedotun Akintola had become very wary of stains.

Despite his religious beliefs, the Commissioner of Police was not able to strike a balance, not where this superstition was concerned. It haunted him every now and then. This superstition shaped his dress code. He developed a passion for neatly-tailored shirts. He was celebrated by his friends, both in the Police Force and in the oil barons' club. He guarded cautiously against stains on his clothes. He just could not bear to think of it. He was contemplating what to do next, when someone knocked on his office door. His secretary walked in.

"Sir, the High Chief is on line two," she said.

The Commissioner of Police was busy brushing off the stained area of his shirt with an handkerchief dipped in soapy water. He raised his head to see the agreeable woman looking at him.

"I heard you," he replied, still struggling with the stain on his shirt.

He became uncomfortable as she just stood there, gazing at him.

"I said I heard you," he almost shouted at her.

"Sir…?" she started, but he interrupted her, "What part of 'I heard you' don't you understand?" he yelled at her.

"The shirt…sir."

"What about it…?" he cut her off again.

"The stain is spreading."

He suddenly stopped to look at the stained area, and noticed the stain had indeed spread. It was almost twice the original size. He walked wearily towards the receiver and snapped it up as the secretary took her leave.

"Sorry to keep you waiting."

The voice at the other end streamed into his ear.

"What?" he suddenly exclaimed.

"When did it happen?" Torrents of questions followed.

"Ok, sir. I will do that right away, sir," the commissioner said.

He took his cell phone and dialled a number. The phone rang at the other end.

"Where the hell has everybody gone?" he started but was interrupted as a voice answered at the other end.

"Hello?"

He exhaled in relief.

"Admiral, sir. The MV Princess will arrive in the next forty-eight hours, requesting your permission to send your boys for inspection, sir."

The Commissioner of Police listened attentively to the Admiral.

"Thank you, sir. All the necessary paperwork will be done once the shipment is confirmed. Thank you, sir."

He grinned from ear to ear.

"Yes sir," he replied to the voice once again.

"Have a nice day, Admiral. Goodbye sir." The commissioner ended the call.

"Oh, God, where the hell can Davis be?" A worried look crept back on his face. He plunged into the swivel chair, and laid his head on the head rest of the chair and gazed into the ceiling, lost in thought. The ringing of the intercom brought him back to reality. He jumped off the chair and grabbed the receiver. The familiar voice of the Deputy Inspector General of Police (D.I.G) came on the line.

"Shaun sir!" he greeted the superior officer.

"Information reaching me says that the MV Princess will berth at shore in forty-eight hours for onward movement to destination?" the inspector asked him.

"Positive, sir," the commissioner responded.

"Conclude all plans for final movement to the final destination," the inspector ordered.

"Yes sir!"

"And forward all reports to me."

"Yes sir," the commissioner responded again,

"And what about the American?" the inspector asked.

"Davis is handling him sir," replied the commissioner.

"Oh, that is good. I know I can count on you. Make sure he is safe. As for the U.S. Ambassador get him ready in case there should be any distraction. I hope there will be none."

"Yes sir. There will be none, trust me," the commissioner confidently added.

"I trust you. See you at the club tonight," the inspector concluded, and the phone went dead. The commissioner bitterly looked at the receiver he was squeezing for the past five minutes, and dropped it in anger.

"I hate taking orders," he fumed. He took a quick look at the stained area on his shirt. "I hope it's not happening again. God, if I pull through this, I will work for a peaceful retirement!" he said to himself.

"Amen," he added to conclude his own selfish prayer. The commissioner stood up, gathered his things together, and walked out of his office.

"I will be gone for the rest of the day. Find Davis and get him to reach me," he ordered his secretary, and left.

Delano, head bowed, was starting to doze off. Tired and weak, tied to a chair in a dark room, Delano tried to free his hands from the ropes that held him bound. He struggled with the rope around his arms. Suddenly a burst of gunfire followed by the sound of bodies falling. Delano desperately tried to free himself but the efforts prove impossible. His hands were firmly tied behind the chair which had served as his uncomfortable home for the past twenty-four hours. The noise outside decreased, and then stopped. He strained his ear for any further sounds, but didn't hear anything. His mind flashed back to Como and the other men in the creeks who promised to watch his back. The door of the holding cell burst open. To Delano's surprise, Davis walked in. He brought out a knife from his jacket pocket and cut the ropes.

"Follow me," Davis ordered, as he walked to the door and peeked outside. Delano tagged along, rubbing his wrists from the pain caused by the ropes. When Delano walked out into the light, his vision became blurred due to his long stay inside the dark room. Davis went ahead, along an iron walkway, stepping over the bodies of assassinated men. Delano tried to keep up with his pace, stumbling slightly as he followed Davis closely. Davis quickly reaches an open exit. Delano, recovering fast, saw a gunman from the corner of his eye aiming at Davis. Suddenly, tumbling towards a dead man on the floor, he spotted a knife on the body and swiftly threw it at the gunman, catching him in the throat. The man dropped to the ground, pulling the trigger of the machine gun he was holding. The explosion caused by the shot drew Davis's attention. He avoided the gunfire and, turning round, discovered the assassin bleeding profusely. Davis looked at Delano with an appreciative glance.

"Let's get out of here!" Davis yelled.

The Commissioner of Police was sitting in the decorated office of the Chief of Marine Affairs, frowning and fuming. The commissioner hated to be kept waiting, and the sudden disappearance of Inspector Davis remained a puzzle. His thoughts were clouded by the flood of events in the last few weeks, since the arrival of Delano. The arrival of the container ship, the MV Princess, and how his retirement plan was about to fall into place. The prospect of a peaceful retirement far from the daily rigours that went with the job, appealed so much to him that, for the first time in weeks, an unforced smile played on his lips, aided by the cool, filtered air from the split-unit AC that hung from the top corner of the office. He was savouring this beautiful prospect, when his cell phone rang, disrupting his thoughts and the silent solitude he was enjoying. After a moment still lost in his thoughts, he overlooked it. He didn't want these thoughts to be disturbed.

The Chief of Marine Affairs walked into the office.

"Hello commissioner!" His greeting woke him up from his thoughts.

"Sorry, the meeting took longer than expected."

The Commissioner of Police found this, a lame excuse for being so late.

"Hope you were well attended to?" the admiral asked, as he walked to place his hat on the office hanger that stood in the right-hand corner of his office.

"Never mind about me, I'm fine," the commissioner replied.

The chief took a seat.

"So to what do I owe this honour? Men like you are rarely seen walking in broad daylight," the admiral said.

"Overlord called to inform me of the arrival of the shipment," said the commissioner.

"What?! Tonight?" exclaimed the admiral.

The commissioner nodded and the admiral immediately got up.

"Must be on my way, got some other people to reach before the day runs out," the admiral responded. They both stepped out of the office and they realised the noon sky had suddenly become dark. The commissioner looked at the admiral and they both smiled.

"The gods of the barons favour us," the admiral said.

"You can say that again. I can't wait for all this to end," replied the commissioner of police.

"Don't be in too much of a hurry, my friend," laughed the Chief of Marine Affairs, patting him on the shoulder.

The heavens opened up abruptly and there was a heavy downpour of rain.

"We will meet at the club tonight," the commissioner said abruptly. The heavily-built, yet unhealthy Commissioner of Police ran towards his car a few cars away. He got in, panting heavily, as if he just ran a hundred-yard dash. The commissioner's driver started the ignition. Gazing at the admiral in the rear-view mirror, he felt sorry for these men. He punched a button, and the window glass slid up. Then, he switched on the air conditioner.

"Thank you, Joey," he said to the driver, a minor concern. By the time Joey turned the vehicle into the Police Force Headquarters, the commissioner was fast asleep. Joey came around with an umbrella, opened the backseat door and tapped him gently. What happened to the once confident officers who started their careers together and came up in the ranks?

"Here we are sir!"

The commissioner woke up, looking dazed gazing at Joey for a moment, trying to remember where he was.

"Oh, my dear," he commented as he dragged his heavy, tired frame from the car. Joey shielded him with the umbrella, and led him into the building. The commissioner went into his office and shook his head sadly. He wondered what his wife would think if she ever knew about all the illegal troubles he subjected them to. The thought of it made him very angry, because he was reduced to errand boy status in his association with the oil barons. He regretted compromising his integrity for power and money. His ill-gotten gains had plunged millions of his countrymen and fellow citizens into a state of unprecedented economic deprivation, poverty and environmental decimation. He looked at his wrist watch and bellowed, "What?!"

It seemed time stood still. He could not wait for the day to run out. He wished for the night to quickly come to an end. The ringing of his intercom rudely interrupted his thoughts. He looked at the phone. It was his secretary. He snatched up the receiver.

"What is it this time?" he roared.

"San-dam is on line four sir. He wants to speak to you," her voice filtered in.

He pressed on a button. "Yes San-dam?"

The voice of San-dam broke the news of Delano's escape to the commissioner who sank low into his chair, speechless.

"Hello, sir? Sir? Are you there?" San-dam demanded.

The commissioner sat motionless, holding the receiver to his ear. Finally, he gently placed it back on the cradle, and lay back in the chair.

Inspector Davis drove into his quiet apartment compound with Delano.

"Make yourself comfortable."

Davis ushered him into his tastefully-furnished apartment. He went into the kitchen, and fetched two bottles of beer. Davis was about to hand one to Delano when a heavy thud echoed from the entrance door. They looked at each other. Davis wondered who the intruder could be. Whoever it was, it must be someone who had trailed him. He motioned to Delano to be still, and tiptoed to the window. He peeped from the side of the curtain blind and saw the commissioner standing there. He immediately told Delano to hide. Delano sprang up and vanished through the door. Another heavy thud fell on the entrance door again. Davis opened the door.

"Sir!" he cried. "What has brought you here?"

The commissioner forced his way inside. Davis closed the door and followed him.

"Sir, you look so worried!" Davis said with a hint of guilt in his voice.

Why shouldn't I be worried!" the man thundered. "The whole world is on my back, the MV Princess is on its way, and the American has suddenly gone missing again, killing all the men on guard and I am just getting the information, and you went missing too! What is happening to everybody and everything?" he yelled.

"Calm down, sir. Calm down."

"Davis, did you just say calm down?" he reacted.

Inspector Davis excused himself, leaving the outraged man standing there. He went into the kitchen, returned with a glass of squash and handed it to him. Delano peeped at the two men from his hiding place.

"Sorry sir, something came up, and I had to leave the town."

The commissioner picked up his bottle from the table. He gulped the drink and sighed. His eyes fell on the other bottle.

"You got company?" he asked.

"Nope…why?" Davis replied.

"Never mind, but you should have called or just sent a message across. You, of all people, should know what I'm going through and how much I depend on you," he said regretfully.

He knew that the success of this mission and his retirement solely depended on the loyalty that remained to be gained from this Inspector Davis. He was still ever so ready to push him as much as he could for his own selfish gain. Davis figured these facts out recently in his encounter with Delano in that dark holding cell. As the commissioner spoke, Davis saw through him and regretted having to break ties with his kinsmen in the struggle for the liberation of their land. How he wished he had really perceived the true character of this old, crafty bastard and his lust for wealth which had led to the betrayal of his kinsmen.

"I'm really sorry sir, it was the urgency of the subject which made me leave town without your knowledge. Now back to this Delano of a guy, what is the news about him?" Inspector Davis inquired.

The commissioner looked confused. "For all I care, that bastard can go to hell. I pray he rots with the militants. I should be thinking of retiring peacefully, if not for all this American interference." Pausing, he sighed and shook his head in misery.

"I warned against the kidnapping of the U.S. Ambassador but nobody would listen to old Adedotun Akintola," he lamented.

"So what do we do now, Sir?" Davis cut in, "The MV Princess arrives tonight."

Akintola gulped the last of what was remaining in the glass and walked towards Inspector Davis. He gripped his shoulders. "The MV Princess is our last chance to walk away, and we will never look back. Help me keep the water guerrillas away, and I promise to make it worth your while."

Davis looked at him sadly, and then lowered his gaze.

"So when does the Princess dock for loading?" Davis asked.

"Come, let me show you." He took his hand and tugged him to the settee. Dipping his hand into his jacket pocket, he brought out a rolled-up paper and spread it over the table.

"This came in before I left the office. It is a detailed information on tonight's operation. This was sent in by the oil corporation."

Davis bent and took a closer look at the plan. "Is that the Cove?"

"Yes, the red pipe will be cut off and the supply sent into the ship. Estimated time of download is thirty minutes. While this is being done, the overlord of the barons will be in the vessel to finalise the arms exchange agreement. Meanwhile, all the Force and crew from the corporation will be on the ground to wade off any intruding force from the boys from the creek. And that is where you come in." He paused and looked at Davis.

"What do you say, son?"

"So what time do they refuel the MV Princess?" Davis asked for clarification.

"The ship will berth at three a.m., local time, and fuel for thirty minutes."

Davis nodded. The commissioner sighed sadly.

"What is it sir?" Davis inquired.

"I needed to hand in Delano by midnight, and that is what I wanted you to do, but now it is becoming a huge task never to be accomplished." He paused and sighed again. "Go around the town, son, and use your contacts. Get me some information," the commissioner demanded.

"Intel from the U.S. reveals Delano is a spy used by the United States Government. The U.S. Government has informed us that Delano is no longer a concern and we must guarantee his disposal while cooperating with the oil barons at the same time. So let him be an accident in the efforts to rescue the U.S. Ambassador, the Police Force will get the credit for the rescue and it is a win, win situation."

"Ok sir, I'll see what I can do." The sound of shattering glass drew their attention.

"What was that?" the commissioner asked in sudden fright.

Inspector Davis dashed to the kitchen. He saw Delano rushing back to his hiding place, grinning at him. Inspector Davis laughed and returned to the living room.

"I'm sorry about that, one of the portraits on the wall fell."

The commissioner nodded and swiftly got up.

"I've got to leave, son, to attend to some other details awaiting tonight's cargo. Please keep me informed about Delano."

"Ok, sir!" he replied. Inspector Davis, who now saw the old man for the brute he truly was, walked him to the door.

An old Passport 90 floated into view from the dense vegetation behind the creek. The sound of the rusty, blown exhaust of the engine sent the guard over. Seeing the jetty on the alert, they all stood and held on to their rifles. The boat sped towards them. They watched the boat gliding to a halt at the foot of the rough wooden jetty. Delano and Davis got out of the boat and walked towards the guard, who stopped them.

"Boss. I want to see your Boss!" Davis demanded. He walked to the barrier, but the guards intercepted him.

"It is important and very urgent," he pleaded with them, but they were unrelenting.

"We must see Como, please," Davis pleaded with them in their mother tongue. One of the guards was angered by his interference.

"You, fucking traitor!" he shouted back at Davis.

"You don't call me names, you, untrained swan!" Davis barked at him.

"You call me untrained!?" the angry guard replied.

"And that is what you are, an untrained fool," shouted Davis, whose ego suddenly overrode the interest of his mission. The guard tried to seize him, but Delano walked in between them. The two men yelled and called each other names. Como came out from the hut and shouted at the guard, suddenly the guard jumped to attention and ran to meet Como.

"What is going on here?" Como asked.

The guard tried to suppress his anger and replied.

"The American came to see you, in company of Davis, and we refused to allow them to go inside," the angry guard declared.

"Let them come!" Como ordered, and he walked back into the hut overseeing the jetty.

"Make way for them!" shouted the guard to his assistant as he walked back to meet the two men. He opened the barrier on the jetty. Delano and Davis marched towards the hut.

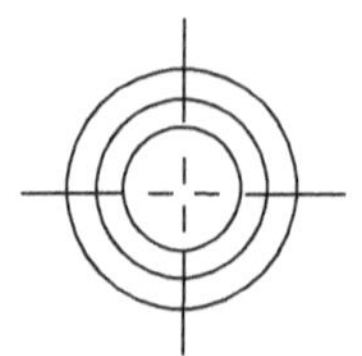

A Reunion

I nside the hut made of compacted bamboo, they discovered a micro conference room filled with smoke from the herb exhaled by Como, who was protected by two guards. He looked disillusioned staring into a blank space. Delano and Davis looked at him, anticipating his next move. On the table a plan was set before Inspector Davis. Como puffed some more from the wrap of marijuana in his hand, and coughed from the choking effect of the smoke. He rose from his chair; his eyes filled with tears because of the intoxicating herb.

"So why should I believe you this time around?" Como finally asked Davis.

"Because of the American," Inspector Davis replied.

"The American," Como said self-consciously and burst out laughing. Delano's gaze was filled with surprise at the sudden sounds of mirth coming from the huge black man. Delano was at loss for words. He didn't understand what they were saying because the two men had spoken in their mother tongue.

"The American freedom fighter is just a stranger to our people. Our intel reports this American is an ex-black militant being used by his government and our leaders. They reap the benefits from our people's resources and destroy our land. They are only interested in their own profits," Como said as he took a drag of the herb in his hand.

"I would prefer that to be left out. Their interest is of no concern to me. So what is of concern to you?" Como asked scornfully.

"His life," Davis chipped in.

"His life… So when did you start to think of people's lives? You, whose actions have killed innocent women and children? You who have raped your own people's land and made them homeless? You, who have worked for the oil cartel which has stolen our God-given wealth? Suddenly you care about life?" Como spat out.

Davis became angry and bitter. Como walked up to meet him and seized him, but Davis resisted him. The atmosphere became tense, choking and Delano decided to interfere, coming in-between them before another fight ensued.

"If not for the American in whose company you have come, you would be dead meat by now!" Como shouted.

"Can someone tell me what is going on here?" Delano demanded, eager to understand what the two men were fighting about. Davis adjusted his clothes and stormed out of the room. Delano ran after Davis. Como banged his fist on the wall. A remorseful look came over him, as he realised that Davis was an important key he couldn't afford to let slip from his hand. Delano caught up with Davis right at the edge of the jetty and held on to his shoulder.

"Davis, don't do this, please!"

"Guess you've seen where we have gotten it all wrong. This is one of the reasons I had to do what I did," Davis explained.

"But now, I'm asking you to do what you have to do for your people, not for Como or his boys," Delano pleaded with him.

Davis' gaze was distant for a moment, thinking about what Delano had just said. He drew in a sharp breath, exhaled and walked ahead of Delano towards the hut. Como was sitting at the table with his head bowed as they entered the hut. Como heard footsteps and raised his head to see both men standing in front of him. He stood up and walked towards them.

"Why are you doing this?" Como asked Davis once again.

"The American has made me realise how much my people need me, and today he saved my life. I just want to tell them how sorry I am about my betrayal," Davis admitted. "I have been so selfish. I have betrayed my countrymen and sold my conscience for a few material pleasures. A country that has seen many of its people die. The pollution, the gas flaring and the horrible squalor of the land."

Como looked at him intently trying hard to believe what he just said. Davis noticed Delano nod and wink at him. Como then inhaled and grabbed Davis' hand. The men shook hands and embraced each other.

"Welcome home, brother," Como whispered to him.

Davis felt warm tears spill from his eyes and his grip around Como tightened.

"I'm sorry," Davis mumbled in a voice laden with emotion.

The scene made Delano want to cry too. Como immediately ordered one of the guards to get food and drinks. The three men exchanged conversations, and when the guard returned, he came back in the company of beautiful girls, with assorted food and drinks.

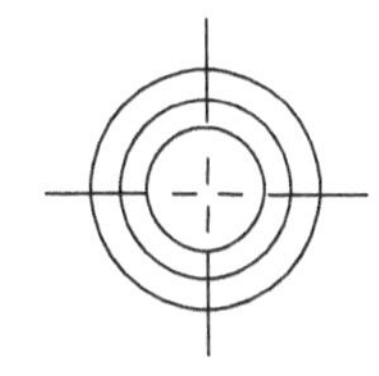

Same Ole Oil

It was late in the evening. The heavy downpour of rain which had disrupted the meeting of the oil barons subsided when the Commissioner of Police arrived, dressed in a white satin suit with an ox-blood-coloured scarf wrapped around his neck. The SUV drove into the parking lot of the state-of-the-art "Empire State" building. In the heart of the city the structure stood magnificently above all other buildings. The view caught the eye of everyone, no matter which part of the city. Its exposure quickly spread, with rumours of corrupt associations. These rumours had in no way deterred these men, and indeed those in high places had continued to hold such meetings. The security network around the building was strong thanks to the huge sums of money provided by the Brotherhood. The Commissioner of Police approached the gate and flung it open. He walked into the deserted reception hall and headed straight for the elevator, and hit the penthouse button. When he entered the penthouse, there was a man sitting on a chair with his back facing the entrance. The smoke from his cigar ascended to the ceiling.

"What is this that I am hearing?" thundered the baritone-voiced man who sat at the other end of the table.

"Your overlord, sir, I don't understand," the commissioner replied shaken, his voice laced with honesty. Immediately the television screen on the wall came alive. The Commissioner of Police recognised the voice streaming from the set, and he turned to look at the screen. He was amazed to see his most trusted man, Inspector Davis in the company of Delano and Como.

"What the hell?" he screamed, bewildered.

"Adedotun?" the man in the chair called out to him.

"Your overlord, sir," he replied with a trembling voice.

"I have worked all my life for this moment, and I know that the Brotherhood has also waited for this moment. So what do you think we should do?" the man addressed him counting on his words.

"Excuse me, your overlord I beg to take my leave immediately." He turned round to hurry out, when the overlord called him back.

"Adedotun?" A deadly silence covered the room.

"Your Eminence," the other replied, tense.

"You know we don't like coming for our own," the voice expressed warningly.

"Please, your Eminence let me take care of the situation."

The Commissioner of Police scurried out. The overlord drew on the cigar tersely, and puffed it up to the ceiling.

The bedroom clock ticked midnight, heralding a new day. It was the dawn of another day. The commissioner's wife tossed and turned on the bed. She awoke, opening her eyes one after the other. The tense figure of her husband pacing up and down, jerked her wide awake. Apparently, he wasn't aware she was awake. He was startled when he heard her call his name.

He turned around swiftly and moved towards her. His gaze softened as he looked at her frail frame lying on the bed.

"Go back to sleep, honey. You need to rest more than ever."

"Your behaviour these days I don't understand. Ade, I'm worried about you. You barely sleep; and even when you eventually do, you wake up suddenly from nightmares. What is going on, Ade?" she asked him.

"Honey, you've got nothing to worry about; I'm fine; everything will be fine," he said, trying to reassure her.

"I have heard these same words repeatedly since the sudden disappearance of the American. Is all really well?"

Her last words got to him. He sensed that she was already suspecting something. Fear gripped him; his heart rate accelerated. He tried so hard to keep her in the dark. He feared that if she got to know about his involvement in the sudden disappearance of the American, this would break her heart, especially now that her health had deteriorated so badly. He did his best to console her.

"Please go back to sleep. Remember what the doctor said. You have to rest more, until he is able to finalise with the hospital abroad, to get you a referral for your operation there." He looked at her with passion in his eyes, and prayed that she went along this last line of reasoning. The feel of her palm against his cheek was reassuring.

"Don't be up too late."

"I won't," he replied, and planted a kiss on her forehead. She went back to sleep. Ade picked his cell phone and dialled it. Someone responded in a low voice. He whispered back, "That's fine, so I will see you soon." The cell phone went dead.

The light of day brightened a narrow corridor leading up the pathway to a faintly-lit cell. An officer walked along the narrow walkway in the company of the commissioner, who ordered him to open the door to the cell. Inspector Davis was awakened by the violent sounds of a club against the iron bars of the cell. He rose from a little mat laying on the bare, broken cement floor.

"Leave us," the commissioner ordered the guard. The guard took his leave. The commissioner looked hard at him and jeered.

"So this is what you've been up to, Davis! Repaying me in such a manner, after all we've been through! Son, I'm sorry, that it has to end like this."

Inspector Davis stood gazing at him with deadly hatred. Venom swelled in his stomach. He wished he could just break through that cage and grab the old bastard and strangle him to death. The commissioner turned. He felt a strong pain in his chest, as he walked out of the hall.

The memories of his short period with Inspector Davis, a man he also fondly called 'My son from another' within the short time he worked with him, left an aching void in his heart. He liked him right from the very moment they met. The emotional pain he felt was so intense; he could only imagine the kind of death that awaited him. Head bowed, the commissioner of walked to the front desk of the prison, took a glimpse at the prison officer, and walked out. He drove off into the night, in his official vehicle. The gate leading to his home opened, and the driver drove the car in silently, switching off the engine gently, as he was instructed, so as not to wake up his wife. Walking inside the bedroom, he made his way up to the wardrobe, pulled off his clothes and tiptoed to the bed. The bedside lamp came on.

"Where are you coming from, Adedotun Akintola Commissioner of Police?" the angry voice of his wife drifted through the room. He came to a halt, shrugged and smiled. He climbed into the bed and drew her gently into his arms.

"Go back to sleep," he said. His wife watched him, puzzled. He kissed her and promptly went to sleep, checking the time. It was three o'clock. She switched off the lamp and they both reluctantly went back to sleep.

The bedside lamp light came on again. The commissioner picked up his wristwatch. and hollered.

"My God," he hollered and got up, tugging his tired body to the bathroom. In a few minutes, he was ready, dressed up for the day's job in his uniform. He took a peek at himself in the wall mirror and took a glance at his wife who was fast asleep.

Ade walked up to her, and planted a kiss on her lips. She stretched and opened her eyes, and saw her husband towering over her. Smiling, she asked in a sleepy voice, "What time is it?" Ade smiled back tenderly at her and answered. "Almost six, dear, good morning. I've got a lot to do today, and so I have to leave early."

He stood up.

"The maid will see to your needs."

He walked out of the room. He settled into the plush seat of his official car His driver drove along the quiet Church Avenue. In the early morning, dew-drenched atmosphere, people rushed to catch their respective means of transportation. The car drove past the hustlers amidst the early morning heavy traffic associated with the city. The commissioner sat straight, contemplating his next move. Prior to his leaving home, he had made a call to Father Innocent Chukwuma, the parish priest in charge of the most prestigious church in the Warri Metropolis, St. Ambrose Assumption Church, which was home to some of the wealthiest men in society, and was run by a man who had gotten a bad name among the other churches.

In fact, most of the hideous crimes committed in society had been repeatedly attributed to the church. Father Chukwuma was still dressed in his nightgown. He paced up and down the altar, rosary in hand, wondering what must have prompted the unusual call. He had known the commissioner for over fifteen years, even before being appointed to St. Ambrose.

Ever since he started his mission at the church, he could not remember the man missing a mass even once. The commissioner never showed any sign of worry, except for the fact that his wife's health had been a nagging problem, since her illness had taken a psychological toll on them. The pressure of his upcoming retirement had also been weighing much on him lately. The priest was trying to figure out what kind of problem could warrant this unholy call. He just couldn't fathom any reason for it. He heard the dying sound of a car engine, went to the pulpit, made a short prayer, and walked to the confessionary.

The commissioner pushed the large double door leading into the huge church and headed for the confessionary. He took a chair by the small window.

"Bless you, my son," Father Chukwuma greeted him.

"Father, I have not come here for confession," he quickly indicated.

"Can we go somewhere else to talk?"

"What is the matter, commissioner?" the priest inquired rather suspiciously.

"Same old oil, same old brothers," the commissioner said.

The atmosphere became strangely quiet. Father Chukwuma sat for a while in silence.

"I will meet you outside," he finally said.

The commissioner sat on one of the benches in the church and crossed his legs. He was becoming agitated, when one of the young servers of the parish entered the church and walked up to him.

"The Father will see you now, sir."

The commissioner stood up and followed him. They walked down the hallway into an adjoining building which housed several rooms built for the church. The young man took the lead. He went up to one of the rooms and stopped. He then beckoned to the commissioner to go inside. He looked at the young, fragile frame of the boy, and placed his hand on the handle of the door. The young boy urged him to go ahead. The commissioner pressed on the door handle, and slowly walked into the room. The priest, dressed in a black vestment, was sitting on one of the couches inside the room that served as his apartment. He offered him a seat. As the commissioner gazed at the interior of the room, the lyrics of Handel's "Halleluiah." Came tumbling into his mind.

Father Chukwuma noticed the awe on his face.

"Come in, please. So what does the Brotherhood want from me this time?" he queried.

"Huh…," he cleared his throat.

"We are expecting a ship." The commissioner tried to explain the situation, but the clergyman cut him short.

"Brother Adedotun, I know the details. What help do you need now?" he asked him comfortingly. The commissioner cleared his throat.

"The MV Princess is at dock as we speak heading for the Escravos River, but the plan has been leaked to the boys in the creeks by one of our most trusted men."

"Inspector Davis!" Father Chukwuma cut in.

"Yes Father, Inspector Davis," the commissioner answered. He continued, "So we have to move the U.S. Ambassador to a much safer place until the business is concluded. I am afraid the guerrilla boys may come for him, because we don't know how much they know, so that is the reason I have come to see you. The overlord said you can come up with something."

The commissioner abruptly came to a halt. The priest gazed at him fixedly.

"Bless you, brother, for all the worries you have gone through. I wish there was something I could do. Right now there is little I can offer."

The countenance of the commissioner changed. The priest leaned sideways, stretched his right hand and picked up a notepad and a pen from the lampstand. He inscribed a few words on it.

"Here, take this." He handed the piece of paper to him, and the commissioner took it from him and read it.

"Take it there. Give it to him. Tell him I sent you," the priest said as he stood up and then walked out of the room, followed closely by the commissioner.

The morning at the riverside was unusually calm, devoid of activity. The air was still which was disconcerting. One could have heard a pin drop on the grass as an uneasy calmness shrouded the atmosphere. Como was dressed in camouflage clothing as he walked along the poorly-lit corridor of the camp house where they carried out various activities for the past three weeks. He opened the door of the large room where they held meetings, and saw Delano with two of his top men. These men stood by him ever since he joined this vigilant group of young men. These young militant groups resorted to taking up arms in the most brutal way. This was the cause of unrest within the oil-rich region.

Como fumed and shouted, "Traitor, I knew he could not be trusted, the slimy bastard!" he said this reference to Inspector Davis, Como took the seat at the end of the table.

"What do we do now?" one of the men asked.

"We will wait until we get a signal from Davis," Delano suggested.

"Did you say Davis?" Como looked and his gaze narrowed dangerously.

"Oyibo, open your eyes, we will be screwed if you and I don't come up with something within the next few hours before midnight."

Como stood up and walked out of the room angrily. Delano glanced at the other two, who looked at him disdainfully. Feeling dejected, Delano hit the table hard, and walked out of the hall, heading straight for Como's room. Delano jerked the door open and saw Como standing at the window looking at the still waters of the creeks.

"I don't really know what you guys are up to. But one thing I do know is that I want to get the hell out of here and carry out my assignment and return home!"

Como turned to face him with an expressionless face.

"We have to strike tonight."

They gazed at each other, speechless for a moment, until Como broke the heavy silence.

"I just got information that there is a party on board the MV Princess. Women have been ordered to come to spice up the party." Como had his eyes fixed on Delano. Both of them smiled.

"I guess we understand what that means?" Como continued and they shook hands.

"I will get the others in on the plan."

Como made his way towards the door. Delano watched him in amazement, overwhelmed by the opportunity.

Twelve hours to deadline, the MV Princess was navigating on the high sea leading to the heart of the oil installations ready for the day's business. The hours were ticking away slowly. Crew members had just put finishing touches to the packaging of the ammo, preparing them for transfer onto the vessel, on her way from the base quarters. The women boarded the MV Princess for the nights party. The chef was also very busy making a variety of food and drinks available. The party had barely started, when the set of PT-90 boats roared away from the camp, carrying a full load of militants.

Meanwhile, Juan Carlos, the Captain of the MV Princess, was sitting in his cabin. He was a rather shabby-looking man, probably in his mid-sixties, a man familiar with the arms and drugs business. He had been in this business for over four decades. A look at him showed years of unhappiness. As a young man he had grown up in the slums of Buenos Aires, Argentina, from a single parent home. He experienced a rough life on the streets. His exploits at the fight club got him a quick ticket up the ranks, and his bravery recommended him to Magnus Vincentia. Magnus Vincentia, the owner of MV Coaster liner International, tutored him in the art of the smuggling business, and later sent him to a school of navigation, where he learnt the skills of sailing. They also enjoyed a long-time relationship with the Brotherhood, which was still unabated even after the military took over the country. Juan Carlos sat there, rather melancholic, with a bottle of red rum in a crystal wine glass on the table. Three of the call girls decorated the little cabin. Having finalised the drug order for the night's business, Juan Carlos settled on the couch, enjoying the caresses from the call girls. His arousal became evident as he enjoyed their erotic touches. All this they did for cash, because Juan Carlos was known for his reckless spending. He didn't hear the bang on the door at first, as he was occupied by his lust. The bang was repeated, and he was startled. Nervously, Juan Carlos yelled, "Ye, coming!" He arranged himself, but found it difficult to settle his manhood which had intensely hardened.

The bang came on the door again. Juan Carlos picked up a pillow and placed it over the stubborn bull that refused to cooperate.

"Excuse me, ladies," he giggled, as he moved swiftly to the door. He yanked it open and yelled, "Who the devil is disturbing my quiet moment?"

Juan Carlos came face to face with one of the crew members.

"Yes, you son of the devil?" he answered angrily.

"The Brotherhood just called. Transactions will take place in a few minutes. They are on in the next fifteen minutes," the man responded, ignoring him.

"Get everybody on deck! I will be with you soon," Juan Carlos replied. And he slammed the door in his face. The crew member just stood there, transfixed, and swore under his breath. As if in a daze, the man then walked away from the lower compartment of the ship housing the captain's cabin. As the crew member was climbing up the staircase, he heard shouts and bizarre footsteps on board the ship. He hastened up the iron staircase. The crew member rose to the top and walked to the door leading outside. When he popped his head out of the doorway, a gun butt hit him on the head. The crew member fell down, lifeless. Two fierce-looking militants moved swiftly down the staircase. They got to the cabin door where a heavy rock tune was playing, a remix titled, "Welcome to the hotel California" by Nigerian and internationally-acclaimed artist Majek Fashek. They banged on the door. The captain flung the door open in annoyance, thinking it was one of his boys again, only to be greeted by the nozzle of one of the militant's rifle. All members on board the MV Princess were tied up by the invading militants and loaded onto a Passport 90, which quickly sped away into darkness.

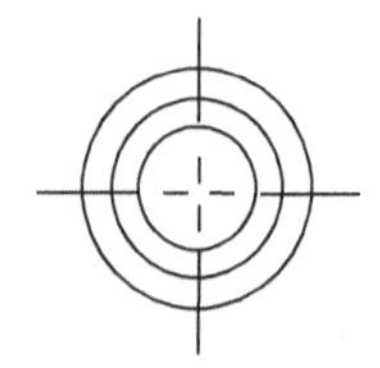

A Bargain

The news of the raid on the MV Princess and the crew taken hostage by militants brought another twist to the events of the past twelve hours. A band of militants made claim to the kidnapping of the crew and the members on board the carrier vessel the MV Princess. The event caused mayhem in the government and private organisations forced agencies to find and prosecute those behind the hideous crime. The Brotherhood were in on covering up the act. The media helped, effectively spreading propaganda about events on the MV Princess. Heavily-built officers and the cell warden walked hastily along the prison corridor. They came to a halt in front of the cell of Inspector Davis. The warden opened the door. The two officers pounced on him and dragged him out. Tugging him to the interrogation room, they tortured him extensively for information concerning his meeting with Como. On the ground, Davis writhed in pain, coughing and bleeding profusely. Then the door to the interrogating room opened and the commissioner walked in.

"Any word yet?" he asked them.

"No, sir."

"Sit him up," he demanded.

They struggled to get him on his feet and sat him on one of the chairs in the room. The commissioner brought another chair from a corner of the interrogation room and sat down opposite him. He looked at him scornfully.

"Like I told you the night I came to see you, I hate all this, after all we have been through together. Tell me what I what to know and who these people are and where I can find them." The Commissioner of Police glared at him. The weak and weary Inspector Davis looked at him foolishly.

"Don't give me that look!" the older Commissioner of Police barked.

"I wish I could make this matter a lot easier for us." The commissioner stood up and ordered them to clean him up.

"You'll be going for a ride," he said and stormed out of the interrogation room.

The two guards yanked Davis off the chair. The patrol cars drove along the expressway leading to the by-pass and the main market. Inspector Davis was sandwiched between two guards who had been assigned to the trip. Inspector Davis calculated his next move. The marketplace was a hub of activities. Traders moved to and fro attending to their daily business. As they drove through, the driver noticed some groups gathering on the road ahead and alerted the other cars. The officer immediately brought the patrol car to a halt. The guards jumped out from the back of the car and went over to clear the way for the patrol car. Davis immediately swung into action. In the blink of an eye, forgetting his wounds, Davis jumped out of the patrol car and ran into the crowd of shoppers and merchants. The officer shouted to the guards, who quickly went in pursuit of Davis. The fugitive ran through the streets among the stalls, hitting traders and knocking down goods. The officers shot at him frantically. Inspector Davis ran, dodging every bullet from the sounds of the gunshots he heard. The officers did not even care about the lives of the innocent bystanders as they shot at Inspector Davis. Davis just ran, heading straight for the riverbank. A fleet of small canoes covered the riverbank, Inspector Davis jumped into one as the guards got to the riverbank and searched for him, unable to find him. The officers returned to face the bitter venom of the Commissioner, who scolded them severely for their failure to secure the only man who knew the hideout of the militants. The same militants who had joined forces with this rebellious American freedom fighter.

He struggled to paddle across the river. Inspector Davis came out of the water after paddling for a long time. Breathing heavily from exhaustion Davis reached the bank of the river with much difficulty and loss of blood. Hands in cuffs, Inspector Davis sat on the riverbank, hardly able to think straight. The first thing he would do was to find a way to get the handcuffs off his hands. But his head was throbbing from pain, and he felt dizzy as he continued to lose blood, bleeding from a wound he sustained from gunshots. As Inspector Davis tried to get up, he stumbled, falling head long and passed out.

In the last few days, the commissioner looked like hell on earth from the terrible pressure he faced as a result of the sudden abduction of the crew of the MV Princess and the escape of Davis. In the eyes of the entire world the Republic had been given a bad reputation. The Deputy Inspector General had already given him a seventy-two-hour window to find those behind the activities. The Deputy Inspector General had planted Adedotun Akintola in the region decades ago to help do the oil barons bidding. The commissioner was hugely rewarded but the Inspector was now throwing him under the bus.

Adedotun Akintola, the Commissioner of Police, faced dismissal now, and to worsen the blow, the Brotherhood concluded his inefficiency did not adequately provide security for the crew of the MV Princess. The Brotherhood threatened to expose Adedotun Akintola as the man responsible, if the Brotherhood was linked to the disappearance of the U.S. Ambassador. Worried and troubled, the commissioner had hardly any time left for his sick wife, who had recently relapsed into frequent comas. All this had also taken a toll on his health, battling with the flu. Despite the drugs his physician prescribed, his state hadn't improved. The business with the Mexicans would have given the Commissioner's retirement plan a great boost but the disappearance of the MV Princess crew had ended those dreams of a smooth transition into retirement.

Those who had paid up for the supplies of ammo were demanding their refund of the money the Brotherhood already spent on other MV Princess transactions. And on top of that no one could find Inspector Davis.

"Maybe he is dead," The Commissioner of Police sighed, not so sure of the true state of his once trusted friend. Though the commissioner feared it, he wished Inspector Davis were dead, as that would be a just reward for his betrayal. The commissioner sat at his dining table, perturbed. He tried to figure out the best way to get out of this debacle. He hated to have ever gotten himself involved in these kinds of transactions right from the start. If he knew the American Government would try to take over in the rescue of the kidnapped U.S. Ambassador, he would have suggested a better means of transaction on the MV Princess. He gazed at the food the house cleaner had placed before him. He was not hungry. He had lost his appetite for anything called food. As he sat there, lost in thought, the house cleaner wheeled his wife into the living room. He saw them and immediately stood up to meet them. He took the wheelchair from the house cleaner.

"I will take it from here," he told the house cleaner. His wife grimaced as she noticed he had not touched his food.

"Dotun, you look worried, my love?"

"I will be fine." he responded, as he wheeled her to a nearby couch and sat next to her.

"I am seeing the doctor today, to finalise the trip," he reassured her.

"Oh, dear, thank you very much, my love." Her face broke into a joyful smile, and tears filled her eyes.

"Things will be better soon, ok?" Ade said softly. She nodded her head, expressing a warm shared feeling. They talked for a while before his cell phone rang.

"Excuse me, dear." He walked up to the dining table where he left the phone and picked it up.

"Hello?"

"Listen carefully, I will not repeat myself," the voice from the other end thundered into his ear.

"Who is this, and what do you want?" The commissioner played the cop he was.

"The bargain will take place at the abandoned Federal Fish Reserve warehouse along the Oporuje Central Market at six in the morning. Come with the U.S. Ambassador. One more thing, your band of untrained officers should back off, or else…"

The phone went dead.

"Son of a bitch!" he exclaimed. His wife, who had been watching him asked, "Is everything alright, honey?"

"Yes, dear, I should be on my way to the office. This idiot will not let me spend time with my lovely wife," he said. He walked to her and planted a warm kiss on her lips.

"Zadora?" he called out. Without waiting, he added, "Whatever you want, Zadora will make it available for you. I will try to be home early today, ok? Love you!" He kissed her again and walked to the dining room table, picked up his keys and headed out the door.

The office of the U.S. Embassy was bombarded by phone calls from the State Department to find out how the search for both Delano and the U.S. Ambassador was progressing. Frantic efforts to get the true position of Delano and the U.S. Ambassador became too difficult for the office. The actions of the Force weighed down with responsibility, yielded little results. Alba was sitting on the front desk, answering phone calls. She looked strained and stressed out. She tried to keep awake by occasionally sipping from the cup of coffee sitting on her desk. She had been charged with the extra responsibility of monitoring all incoming calls. Toyin, her colleague, had stopped coming to work. The office at the American Embassy had become tense, since all the workers had been on the receiving end of the pressure mounting on the ambassador. The constant barking and shouting at office staff by the big man had gotten to such a crescendo that some of the local staff engaged with the services of the American Embassy hardly came to the office. Most of them could no longer stand the harassment from the Americans. The whole place looked deserted, except for the few American workers who still worked there. Since the incident, the ambassador barely left his office. On that fateful day, he sat on his chair, looking dejected and forlorn, contemplating his next move. The pressure from the State Department Security was threatening his career. The phone on his desk buzzed. He reluctantly bent towards it and pressed the answering button.

"Yes, Alba?" he answered passively.

"It's Delano, sir. He demands to speak to you."

The mention of Delano's name sent the man reeling off his chair.

"Put him through to me!" he ordered.

"Ok, sir."

He couldn't wait for the call to come through.

"Ahoy, sir" Delano's voice hailed him at last.

"Where the hell have you been, son?" he asked with a sigh of relief.

"I will pretend I didn't hear that, ambassador," he replied.

"Don't get smart with me, where are you?" the ambassador responded.

"Is the line safe to talk?" Delano asked.

"Hold on a minute." He placed his palm over the mouth piece. "Alba, transfer the call to Alpha 01," he commanded.

Alba stood up and ran to the exchange panel, then pressed a button.

"You are onto Alpha 01 now, sir," she informed him.

"Go on, Delano."

"I am in the creeks with…," Delano started.

"You are what?" the ambassador exclaimed.

"I'm safe, sir."

"How well do you know these people?

"I have spent four years here. I think it is enough time to know… why all these questions, son?"

"There will be a haggle tonight…"

"Hag what!" exclaimed the ambassador.

"You heard well, sir. So I should speak with the presidency immediately and ask for… I have to go! I will contact you again." The phone went dead.

"Delano! Delano!" he shouted into the mouthpiece. Delano was gone.

"Damn you, Delano" the man commented.

"Gosh!" He threw his fist to the air, picked up the phone, and called Alba.

"Get to the Deputy Inspector of the Force, right now!"

A few seconds later, the phone rang again. He feverishly pressed the receiver button.

"The Inspector on Alpha B, sir," Alba informed him. The ambassador switched off the set and turned over to Alpha B.

"Inspector," he said, apprehensive, not even remembering to greet him.

"Inspector, I need assistance with some of your men."

"For what purpose?" the inspector asked, taken aback.

"I know I can count on you, inspector?" he inquired.

"Oh, sure ambassador," the other affirmed.

"Delano is alive…"

"What?" the officer exclaimed. "Alive? Where? How?"

"That I can't explain now, but he called me a moment ago." The ambassador sighed and continued, "He promised to call back. He needed help. He mentioned a haggle."

"Haggle what…?" the inspector exclaimed, "With whom and where?" he asked, astounded.

"The only thing I know is there is going to be one. I have no idea where and who is involved. He will be calling back. By then I expect I'll get the information. I am positive he needs help."

"It depends on what kind of help he needs. As for men, I can make them available," the inspector assured him.

"Thanks inspector, I knew I could count on you, my dear friend. I will get in touch with you, once the picture is made clear," he promised. The Inspector dropped the receiver, picked up his cell phone and dialled Adedotun's number. The phone rang, but no one picked the call.

The guard manning the access of the locally-made jetty which led to the militants' stronghold where the crew of the MV Princess were held hostage had dosed off on his chair. His legs lay on top of the wooden bamboo tree used to build the bridge. The roaring sound of a fast-moving Passport 90 woke him up. He stood up and cocked his AK 47 rifle. Stationed at the head of the bridge, he kept watch on the boat.

A robust boy in his early teens, wearing only shorts, and drenched all over, waved and shouted in the Ijaw language.

"They shot him, they shot him!"

He approached the bridge and brought the boat to a halt. The guard took a peek at the half-dead Davis who lay on the floor of the boat. He raised an alarm, shouting in the local vernacular too. Immediately streams of other militants rushed out; Delano in the company of Como came out. The guard and the young boy carried Davis into the house.

"Bakumor, assist them and take him to the bay," Como ordered.

Bakumor ran out of the group, handed his rifle to a mate, took Davis from the boy and carried him inside. Followed by Delano, Como came to Davis who had been laid on the bed made of sticks and dressed with cloth. Como asked Bakumor in his native language to go and fetch some herbs. The man ran out of the room; Delano looked at Davis, silently writhing in pain. He turned to Como.

"He needs the attention of a doctor," he told Como.

"He will be fine," Como assured him. Bakumor returned with some herbs.

"Prepare it!" he ordered him.

Bakumor drew out a plate from underneath Davis's bed. He emptied the content of the bag into the bowl and ground the herbs vigorously for a few minutes. He finally came to a stop, breathing heavily.

"Apply it to the wound!" Como ordered.

Bakumor put some of the roughly ground leaves on the wound on Davis's shoulder and rubbed it in. Davis groaned in pain.

"He will be fine," Bakumor declared.

Delano looked at Como in disbelief.

"Will he be alright?" he asked. But he received no answer. Bakumor finished dressing the wound, stood up and left the bay. Delano watched Davis as he slowly slipped into a half-conscious state, almost as if he had fallen asleep from the effect of the sedative contained in the herbs.

The night that followed the rescue of Davis was terrifying. He fell into a coma twice after a very serious convulsion. Twice he fainted, and twice he was revived; his condition became somewhat stable.

Bakumor had to come back and see to his welfare. It was three in the morning, and Bakumor had fallen asleep due to exhaustion from making Davis' condition stable. He did not realise Davis had woken up. It was the sick man's cry, a strange sound which Bakumor thought sounded like 'Delano' that woke him up. His eyes still filled with sleep, he dragged his feet on the floor to Delano's room and gently tapped on the door. Delano came to the door and placed his ear on it.

"Who is it?" he queried.

"Bakumor."

Delano opened the door.

"Davis…," Bakumor paused.

"Yes, what about Davis?" Fear gripped Delano. His eyes were filled with fright as he waited for Bakumor to speak.

"He wants to see you," he replied.

Immediately, Delano picked up his shirt and dashed out with Bakumor.

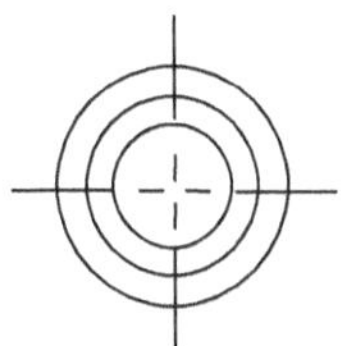

A Clandestine Operation

The days that followed the rescuing of Davis proved worrying for the commissioner and the ambassador. Neither of them was contacted by the faction. The news of Davis' escape and the kidnapping of the crew of the MV Princess had leaked into the stealthy ear of the press, who had been looking for breaking news ever since the Delano issue had caused a lot of misgivings that threatened the bilateral relationship between Nigeria and the US. The US Senate ordered the recall of the ambassador, citing incompetency in protecting American citizens as the official cause for it. The ambassador desperately needed to hear from Delano during the short time he was allotted. He spent most of his time in the office, waiting for news from Delano.

The camp of the band of jungle friends was thrown into confusion and fighting. Delano came to meet the half-trained militants whose lack of modern medicine and experience, and the negligence of human lives had cost Davis his life. His death stalled their planned haggle, which was supposed to take place the night before. Armed with the information that Davis had found the strength to confide in him, Delano threatened to go on a solo course to find and rescue the U.S. Ambassador. He was quietly putting his belongings together and dressing up to take his leave, when the door of his room opened, and Como walked in. Seeing Delano dressed up, he took the hint.

"I know you must be angry. Anyone would. It has never happened before. That is why we didn't think it necessary to get a better treatment for him. Moreover, all the other gun wounds have been treated here."

Delano ignored Como, who pleaded with him in a voice laden with emotion.

"You have the right to be angry…."

"I am not angry!" he thundered back at him. "It won't change anything. It's just that my head is clear now. I think I have to be on the move and fulfil my mission, with or without your help," he stated with a bitter taste of disappointment.

"And… our unfinished business?" Como asked, trying not to aggravate his mood further.

"We haven't got any unfinished business," Delano replied with an expressionless voice.

"What about Okitoro?" Como chipped in. Delano stopped packing his personal effects and looked at him with eyes red with rage and disgust that sent a chilling sensation down Como's spine.

"This has got nothing to do with Okitoro."

"And the pact you promised him before his camp was razed?" Como was trying to get an alibi. Delano immediately felt limp, as if strength had just been drained out of him. He paused and sat on the bed beside his luggage. Como glanced at him from the corner of his eyes, a satisfied feeling flooded him as he saw the effect his reminder was having on Delano. He sat down on the bed beside him.

"I heard you," Delano added and sighed. "Davis shared a secret before he died."

Como looked at him with surprise and nodded his head.

"I don't know what you, people, talked about, but I know it has to do with the U.S. Ambassador." Their gazes locked.

"Delano, you could be our only chance to let the world know our stance in this struggle. You can't afford to turn us down now."

His patronising and soothing voiced echoed in Delano's mind. Como stood up abruptly and walked to the door. He opened it slightly and turned around to face the American.

"Delano, let's do this together."

Delano raised his head slowly, and saw Como's shadow pass through the door. The door closed gently behind him. And then Como heard Delano's voice again.

"What is this?" Como walked back into the room. He saw Delano holding up a seal with his left hand. He went over and collected the seal from him. Como looked at it intently, as Delano gazed at him.

"He gave it to me, I mean Davis."

"I don't know much actually," Como, relieved, explained to him.

"It belongs to the cartels running the big oil business on our soil; those in high places who have shared the wealth drawn from the region without any concern for the development of our land."

Como paused. "But why did he give it to you?"

"I don't know! It is not the first time I have seen this. The girl at the club and Preye, all had some sort of connection with this seal."

"What seal?" Como asked.

"This." Delano raised the emblem of oil dropping from a barrel. Como looked at the seal. He turned it round and read out the inscription at the back. "Flight Road -Well 57 Olobiri 20th Street Staac Wwr".

"I think it is a date on a monument or something like that," Delano said in an inaudible voice, laden with consternation that the news of Davis's death had brought over him.

"I need to know what this inscription stands for."

Como, puzzled, looked intently at the emblem.

"Olobiri is an exploration site in the deep waters over the Escravos oil facility, and was the first ever exploration site in the region." He paused then murmured the word. "Well 57" and thought for a while. Delano kept his eyes fixed on him, racking his brain to figure out what the inscription before his very eyes.

"57 could mean...That was the year!" he suddenly uttered.

"Yes, the year! 1957 was when the first oil well was discovered in the region Flight Road, 20th Street Staac." Como was engrossed with working it out.

Delano swiftly moved towards the pillow on the bed that had served as his comfort zone since his arrival here with this band of friends. He could not guess what they really wanted from him. All he wanted was to get going in his rescue mission of the U.S. Ambassador. He came back, holding a small diary bounded with a rubber band, apparently also given to him by the late detective Davis. He flipped through the pages of the small book, as if he knew the answers to the question at hand. Both men in the room seemed to have found a common ground; preoccupied with the immediate task of finding out the meaning of the inscription and the code.

Both of them were striving hard to figure out what was encrypted on the seal. It was the key. Delano's intuitive mind was the first to come up with a possible clue to the remaining part of the unsolved code. He asked rhetorically.

"What moves in the air?"

"Planes of course," Como replied reflexively, without paying heed to what he just heard. But his reply just threw more light on the hidden clues of the encrypted inscription.

"Flight road, plane road," murmured Como.

Delano was now pacing up and down the small room. His military-trained brain was put to the test. He had acquired the psychometric training of a Marine Officer working with the Federal Bureau of Investigation (FBI), before his unit was sent to Iraq; war which saw Saddam's government toppled by the Americans and the allied forces, in the wake of the renewed hostilities of the gulf war in 2000. While he yet pondered, his mind fell on a host of possibilities. He turned to Como and asked.

"Is there any airport in the surroundings?"

"My God," exclaimed Como.

"Why did I not think of that before?" Delano looked at him quizzically.

"Come, follow me!" he ordered.

Como practically dashed out of the room, with Delano running after his heels.

The priest was sitting in his study, preparing his weekend sermon. Respect for the Church and political circles, was one thing he always nurtured, but this had suddenly started to wane. The rumours of his nefarious activities with the Brotherhood had become an issue of contention among the heads of the other parishes. The priests had repeatedly petitioned the Bishop to transfer him from St. Ambrose

Assumption Church to another one, citing, to justify their demand, connivance with the political class that regularly aided the multinationals and the oil barons in perpetuating injustice in the region. Most of these angry priests were ignorant of the fact that the very Brotherhood that had infiltrated the religious circles was responsible for the shots right from the top through their unalloyed support for the Church. Worst hit in this polity-religion marriage were the Pentecostal churches; as his flagging figure within the society was dwindling due to the recent attacks from his co-brothers in the Lord's circle.

The Brotherhood of the Oil Barons had rallied support for the priest by continually impressing it on the bishopric that they should continue to keep him at St. Ambrose's Church for as long as they required his services. Otherwise they would be forced to withdraw their support for his candidacy to the post of Archbishop which he was presently running for.

Father Chukwuma was seated engrossed in his reading, when the sharp ringing tone of his cell phone rudely interrupted his concentration. He saw the blinking, alert text message from the commissioner on his phone. He immediately read through the content.

"As earlier discussed, Most Reverend Father, the Brotherhood has ordered the immediate relocation of the consignment. It is believed that the consignment has been grossly compromised" He finished reading the message and deleted it without a second thought. He hated the idea of a common, carnal man dishing out orders to him. He often reasoned that 'mere man' without the calling of God should instead receive orders from him. But selling out his spiritual conscience to the Brotherhood for the prospect of money; real money, as he often called it in times past, was what the just longed for. The only reason why he decided to go into priesthood was because he loathed the thought and sight of poverty.

As a young man whose father's poor status had constantly turned him off, he was forced to compromise his genuine interest for the faith. He felt pain and remorse in his heart that he stood on the altar, time and time again deceiving the body of Christ. He continually begged for a second chance from the Almighty. This, his heart told him, would happen neither in this life, nor in the life to come. So he planned to make a complete turnaround, by publicly confessing his wrongdoing to the entire congregation. The thought of it, sickened him to the bone; he couldn't bring himself to do what he knew was right. He abandoned his pre-prepared sermon and walked out of the study with a heavy heart. The sensation he felt spelt trouble. He guessed that allowing the commissioner to place the U.S. Ambassador under his own care was not the best decision he had lately taken. Especially now, when both the national and international communities were fast becoming interested in the case of the Niger Delta, which had come to the fore because of the bands of untamed Guerrillas.

When the Guerrillas had started this agitation for the development of their region and the controlling of their natural resources, they had opened a can of worms which now threatened the fundamentals in which the Brotherhood was anchored. How he wished the late despot had not killed the erudite writer and activist Ken Saro-Wiwa, who knew how to fight a battle by employing all diplomatic means in the struggle! The father remembered how the windfall from selling the crude oil had brought him favour in cash and kind, whenever he assisted the Brotherhood in subverting the truth. Their own truth he often propagated among his numerous members and seminar attendants. But he bemoaned how his white robes had helped to fool a lot of people who could not see beyond the cassock. In the hall of the church, he went straight to the altar and knelt down to offer the prayer of one whose gross sin needed the forgiveness of the Almighty. His greed had put him in harm's way with God.

The office door of the late detective Davis flung open, and Delano walked in with Banga. The nicely arranged room drew a sharp contrast with the late detective's shabby frame before he passed on. Delano ordered the immediate search of the apartment for something he couldn't quite place yet; except that they seriously sought any information that would lead to the whereabouts of the kidnapped

U.S. Ambassador. They looked all over the apartment; turned everything upside down, yet they couldn't find anything. Banga's phone suddenly rang. He took it out from the pocket of his camouflage waistcoat. The voice of Como drifted into his ear.

"Ensure immediate withdrawal from the premises. You guys are being closed in on by some unidentified operatives."

Banga cut off the line in a hurry and turned to Delano. "We have to leave right now! They have located us and are closing in on us."

Then he walked towards the door, leaving Delano whose cop instincts told him he was close to finding something; something he couldn't place his hand on. But he was convinced that what he was seeking for was here; close by.

The heavy iron-gate leading to the apartment creaked. The sound alerted the two men. Delano rushed towards the drawer table housing the set of LG electronics gadgets. He lifted the DVD player and, bingo, his eyes fell on files with a neat inscription "Davis". He turned and looked at Banga who was mounting guard at the door. With a nod of the head, Delano ordered for their immediate withdrawal from the apartment, just in time to escape through a door leading to a closet which Delano had discovered while they were searching the apartment. At first sight, no-one could easily guess that there was such an accessible door there. It took the smartness of Delano to figure it out. The door was walled-in to suit the frame of the wall, and the blended colours served as a clever disguise. They squeezed through the door and shut it silently behind them, as they could hear the footsteps of the intruders assaulting the apartment. A moment later, certain that they were not in the apartment, one of the three officers—apparently the leader of the group—brought out a phone and searched for a contact.

"Target not found. Nothing seems to be missing. The whole area has been swept clean for possible evidence of missing items. Team is leaving to join the rest of the search team. "Over and out." The officer then heard the depressed voice.

"Boys, let's move out," he ordered. Immediately they all filed out of the apartment. Delano and Banga peeked through the curtains and saw the officers moving out. They quietly came out of the providential closet.

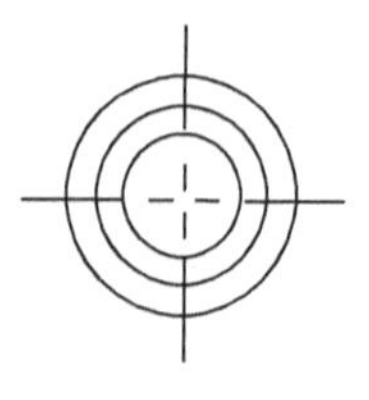

Caution

The Brotherhood held another meeting to discuss the recent developments of the hostage affair. Recent records showed that the numbers ran into hundreds of thousands of dollars. An informant within the presidency alerted the Brotherhood of the decision of the President to immediately disband the Joint Force put in place in the wake of the ugly incident that had degenerated into chaos in the region, and set up a new operational team to find the kidnapped U.S. Ambassador and the crew of the MV Princess. This action, if allowed to take place, would spell doom for the Brotherhood, as most of them had practically lost all their savings in the new business of power sabotage and fuel subsidy, something a lot of Nigerians had frowned upon, calling for the probe of these ministries.

The Brotherhood feared the new directives that the President would soon enforce. It meant that some of the trusted men they had set on the trail of the American would now be compromised, and this, they could not allow to happen. They had assured their business partners that they would do everything to secure the release of the kidnapped crew of the MV Princess, and definitely seal the drug deal which the kidnapping had forestalled. The members were seated. The most reverend man of the course on ground walked into the meeting. The rest stood up to herald his coming. With a wave of his hand, he allowed them back on their chairs. He sat down and examined the events of the day.

"Gentlemen, Brothers, trusted allies and friends, in the wake of the pursuit of a better living for future generations, it appears that we have been compromised by some groups whose demands have blindfolded the very existence of this group…" He watched the sea of still faces to make sure he wasn't talking to himself. Certain he had their attention, he continued, "...which over the years has single-handedly brought successive governments to power, run their errands and done their bidding. Now is the time for us to ask for a little favour in return for all these years of service. And what do we get?" He again paused and looked at the faces of the men who had financed the big oil business, to the detriment of those whose lands had been stolen, without remorse and concern for the people's plight. He noticed their weary looks but continued.

"A government we have paid heavily to bring it to power is threatening to remove food from our table. This is unacceptable." The Brotherhood murmured their support, according to this characteristic method of lording it over the bunch of bigots who had impoverished the people of the region for their selfish interests.

He continued again, "In front of you is a plan of action we intend to carry out in days to come, and this is aimed at the Bongola facility on the high sea. Be aware that through this action there will be a great loss, the kind that has never been heard of in this country. But know this, that when this action finally materialises, this puppet in power will have no cause but to disband the Joint Task Force. Rather he will immediately call for the beefing up of the existing unit of the Joint Task Force, which is made up of some of our trusted allies. This means that our men will invariably continue to run the show and the manhunt for the release of the MV Princess crew. And that will set us up for the conclusion of our business."

He paused and smiled with an air of satisfaction. "This will not only help to cushion the effect of the loss this immediate attack has caused us, but also triple our wealth." He paused again and looked around. "Before I end this express executive meeting, I want to warn you that these are dire times. We all should do well to reassess our finances and be prudent, and make sure our international counterparts are not relenting in supporting our cause." These reassuring words from the efficient leader set the minds of those present in the meeting at rest. The events of the past few weeks had actually not only weakened their trust and resolve in the Brotherhood, but some of them had also suffered financial setbacks. As the meeting concluded, they left with a renewed hope and belief in their leader, who had successfully run the affairs of the powerful oil Brotherhood for more than three decades.

Delano sat quietly on his bed, his head buried in the documents scattered there. He was so much engrossed in studying them that he missed Como walking in.

"Any luck with what you're looking for?"

Como's question startled him. He raised his head after another look at the most priced item on the list he had so far gone through. Watching Como, he thought to himself.

"This fucking nigga has no idea how badly he is in demand."

"Is there anything wrong?" Como asked, as he was surprised by the anxiety written on his face.

"Come, take a look at this." Delano handed him one of the documents.

Como read it and yelled, "What, where, when is it taking place?"

"I guess the answer is here." Delano handed another piece to him. Como gazed at the abbreviated letters and was astounded by what they meant.

"STAAC" – St. Ambrose Assumption Church.

"Jesus!" he exclaimed. St. Ambrose, Airport road, Flight road. The words rushed to him in chorus, "Father Chukwuma! My God!" He stood there, stunned.

"Yes, I think the answer to that plot lies with that person in question."

Como looked so serious; he fumed with anger. He paced up and down the room. Delano looked at him and tried to read his mind, but his inability to know what was on the other side of the brain of the self-acclaimed leader ordained by the Spiritual Head of the Egbesu, sent jitters down his spine.

"What's on your mind, C.O?" Delano chose to use his title of Commanding Officer to soften him up.

"This must not be allowed to happen," Como spat out. "The success of this operation will be the end of my people, because the government will embark on a reprisal attack on us, thinking we are behind it." He walked to Delano, who was endeavouring to come to terms with what he was saying.

"You must help us now, or else we are going to be doomed for reasons that are certainly not our fault. All we are asking for is the development of our land, as they have done to the Federal Capital Territory (FCT), Abuja. There, they provide huge sums of money on a daily basis from the exploration of our God-given natural resources; to send our children to school and educate them to face the future challenges; provide us with a better environment devoid of pollution and degradation of our farmlands, which have long been our standing means of livelihood for our people down in the creeks; give us better health care, good roads, industries to employ our graduates; create a better, empowering environment for small scale businesses, stop the gas flaring…"

Delano cut him off, "Wow, wow. Slow down, man, I don't quite understand what you are saying." He smiled at the man, stunned at his desperate passion for his people. "This is not my country, you know."

Como came and sat beside him on the bed and sighed.

"This struggle is not a premeditated one. It started spontaneously as a result of what happened to one of our communities, called Odi, after a series of attacks that rose from communal crises among various ethnic groups."

"Odi?" Delano asked in his American accent.

"Yes Odi. In the year, 1999, some of our brothers were framed up on the trumped-up charge of disrupting the activities of the multinationals. The Federal Troops were sent by Olusegun Obasanjo, a former civilian president, to counter them. During the raids, the community of Odi was reduced to naught. The soldiers killed innocent civilians and children. Our women and mothers were raped in broad daylight, and pictures taken by these renegade Federal Troops were displayed on national dailies worldwide. All this happened despite the calls from international NGOs. Prominent among them was, Amnesty International. They proceeded to prosecute all those behind the massacre at Odi. But to date, no group; not a single soul, neither in private circles nor in public ones, has been brought to book."

While Como was narrating the story of the Odi fiasco in 1999, images of how the Taliban had killed civilians and raped innocent woman and girls during the uprising in Iraq and Afghanistan, before his unit was sent in to help rescue those that were held captive, flocked to Delano's mind.

"Now that the government is doing everything possible for us to place our cards on the table so that amnesty can be granted us, even though we don't really know the terms of the government's amnesty, it is something we want to embrace. And watch out how it plays, Mr. Martins…," he warned. Delano's eyes beamed with surprise. He never imagined that any of them knew his second name, because no one had ever addressed him by his beloved name ever since he was forcefully transported here by Okitoro, before his supposed untimely death at the hands of the Joint Force group.

"You see, that is why this plot in the port of Bongola should not be allowed to take place. If it is, then the government will bring everything they have at hand to accuse us. And they'll do their best to make life unbearable, not only for our people, but for your people and other foreign nationals."

Delano stood up and walked over to the table top refrigerator. He took a can of beer. Opening it, he gulped half of its content and exhaled.

"Sorry, man, I can't help you on this. I just want to get going on the U.S. Ambassador and get the fuck outta here. I think I have gotten myself involved too much in your stuff, and long enough. I have given you the best help I can, that is making this plot known to you. Now I'll set out tomorrow for the rest of my mission." He gulped the rest of his drink, and walked out of the room. Como, lost in disappointment, stood watching him, until he was gone. All of a sudden, he started to notice some mist covering the whole room. He crouched; face bowed. Then a voice from the mist with thunderous lighting said, "Be patient."

The words echoed, the sound filling the whole room, and faded out. The mist was gone in the twinkle of an eye. Como nodded in reverence, stood up and walked out.

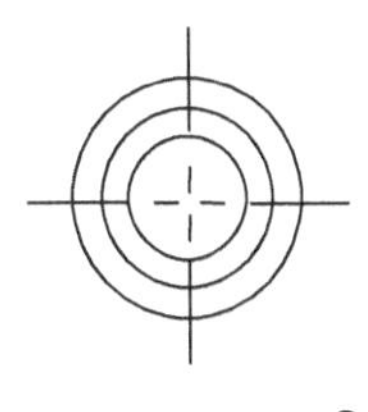

The Bait

The evening sun was beginning to set on the horizon, immediately giving way to the early signs of the night. The worshippers at St. Ambrose's Assumption Church were gathering for the usual late evening mass. Half an hour later, the last of the worshippers walked through the heavy metal gate that shielded the mass of the edifice from the glare of society. The gate attendant was closing the gate, when suddenly he heard a bang on the steel door. Opening it, he popped his head outside. A man in a flawless white cassock stood there.

"Good evening, Father," the gateman greeted him with all reverence. Is Father Chukwuma in?" the man asked the gateman, who was of a much advanced aged and looked untidy. Then, he walked past him into the Church premises. At that moment, three men quickly rounded up the gateman and sent him to sleep. One of them applied a firm hold on his neck and quietly dragged him inside the security room. The four men advanced straight towards the Cathedral.

Two of them kept watch at the entrance door, while Delano and Shaka entered the main hall of the church building. Father Chukwuma was finishing his evening job before retiring to his room, when he caught a glimpse of the white cassock. He immediately abandoned what he was doing and went out to meet them. But much to his dismay, they grabbed him violently. He immediately started to protest; the one thing that crossed his mind was that he was being kidnapped. They silently forced him out of the building. Outside the gate, a Range Rover car sped up towards them and came to a halt beside them. Again, they forced the protesting man into the car and drove off, into the distance. The Range Rover came to a warehouse on the outskirts of the town. Two of the guards came out and closed the doors, leaving them in complete darkness as the lights of the car went off. Delano looked for a switch and eventually found one. Immediately, the whole warehouse came alive as he turned on the lights.

"Take him out!" Delano ordered. He walked towards the SUV car and the other two men who had embarked on the mission brought out the priest who was blindfolded. Pushing him hard, he fell to the floor. Delano walked up to him.

"Oppressor man!" he yelled at him.

"Please, don't harm me! I beg you in the name of God! Whatever you want, I will give it to you," the priest whimpered.

"I am going to remove this blindfold from your face. But I swear that, if you make any false move or any attempt to shout, I will break your neck. Do you understand what I just said?" The priest nodded in quick affirmation.

He was ready to do whatever it took to gain his freedom back; even though he was not sure what his captors had in store for him. A million thoughts ran through his mind. The dark blindfold came off his face, and he struggled to get his eyes accustomed to the strange surroundings; at least to see the faces of his captors. Haziness and blurry vision gave way, and he could see clearly again. A quick scan of his new environment killed his hopes of any immediate rescue. His gaze roamed from one heavily-built, armed man to the next, until his eyes fell on Delano, who had all along been standing next to him, looking intently at him.

"Delano!" Father Chukwuma exclaimed.

"So you know my name!" he replied dryly.

"They say you are dead!"

"Let's just say, I'm Jesus, you know, who rose from the dead, or I'm just a ghost of the Holy Ghost dogma." He snapped his fingers, and one of the men brought forth some documents. He took them from the man, who then walked back to take his position.

"I'm going to show you a map, and you know what? I will appreciate it if we make this easy, so that those you love will not be made to suffer. You know, before I came for you, I have already established the fact, that you and a few individuals are not actually who you claim to be. A priest who is in a cult; who kills and maims people, and the dark secret you have—you fathering children, which is against the oath you swore to keep, imagine what all these facts would do to your career! If ever you come out of this alive…"

"What is it you want from me? Tell me and I will oblige you! Please, don't do what will ruin the reputation I have built all through these years," the priest pleaded, cutting Delano off.

"Reputation?" Delano chuckled disdainfully. "Ok, oppressor man." He opened the map before him.

Father Chukwuma looked at the map. "I don't know anything about this map. I haven't even seen it before," he answered.

"Are you sure? Really sure, I mean?" Delano asked him amusingly. He nodded his head in the affirmative.

Delano beckoned to one of his men. The guy walked up to him, carrying an iPod. As he got to him, Delano ordered him with a nod of his head to do what had to be done.

The guard pressed on the play button of the iPod. An aged woman's voice issued forth in Igbo, pleading with them, amidst crying, to spare her life. Hearing and recognising the voice, the father burst into tears.

"Please, don't hurt my mother! She is the only one person in the world I have left," he appealed to Delano and the men around him.

"That will not happen, if you oblige us with what we want, and that depends on how fast you are willing to do so." Delano added. And he stared at him. Reaching for his breast pocket, he brought out the stick of a squeezed cigarette, cut off a bit of the tobacco and threw it into his mouth. He chewed on the substance, with a face which indicated he did not like the flavoured substance. He tightened his lips as he bent down to the father.

"So what have you got to say about this?" He tapped on the map spread on the lap of the priest, who gazed down and then raised tear-filled eyes to look at Delano.

"Please, believe me for all I'm about to tell you. What I am going to say is all I know about this map." Delano looked at him intently, indicating that he should go on.

"There is going to be a pull out on the Bongola port, but the time and date I don't know. If there is anybody that can tell you anything about this map, then that will be the commissioner"

"Dirty old bastard," Delano swore under his breath.

"All I can tell you is that they will make it look as if the boys in the creeks were responsible for the take out, an action that will now make the government come after them. It will provide a leeway for the exportation of massive crude products, which will be given in exchange for the drug and terrorism business which they are presently masterminding in the north of the country. They hope this will help checkmate the insurgents of the militancy in the Delta."

"What about the U.S. Ambassador? Who are those who hold him hostage?" Delano asked. The priest looked at him and fear crept into his face. He hesitated.

"Did you hear the question I just asked?" Delano forcefully insisted.

His eyes still filled with fear as he continued, "When you came and got involved with the militants, the commissioner, through Davis, moved the U.S. Ambassador into my custody, and he was kept safe until the advent of Davis' betrayal, which they feared could jeopardise their mission of making the world believe that the militants were responsible for his kidnapping. And they had planned it right from the onset. Once the authorities were after the militants, they would have an easy route and access to welcome the MV Princess, which was supposed to bring in the first large scale shipment of drugs and devices to make bombs. This would launch a new phase of regional struggle in the country, a struggle aimed to distract the presidency from their agenda of reforms in the Niger Delta. But the seizure of the ship's crew has delayed this plan. That is why the Bongola Port attack is now placed above any other plan on the business radar. So the commissioner came and ordered the immediate relocation of the U.S. Ambassador from my care."

"So where is he likely to be held now?"

Delano asked, trying hard not to betray his emotion.

"I don't know! If there is anyone who has any knowledge about that, then that would be the commissioner himself."

"I hope all you have said is true, because if I find any false information, I will personally track you down." Delano bent down and looked at him closely. "Do you understand what I've just said?" he asked again.

The priest nodded in the affirmative. Delano beckoned to one of the three boys. The young man walked to him and brought a mobile phone which he handed over to the priest.

"Now you have got to call the commissioner and tell him to meet you in church in two hours."

The priest took the phone, and without a second thought, dialled the commissioner's line.

Waiting for so long for Delano's call had caused the commissioner to grey almost overnight. He wondered what game the crazy American was playing this time around. To make things worse, the government quarters had made repeated calls to enquire about the sudden disappearance of the crew of the MV Princess. The Special Task Force had been called in to take up the immediate investigation. That morning was rather a disturbing one. Over three decades of marriage, not once had he raised his voice at his wife. Sitting in his office, he was worried and disturbed over the incident that had taken place at home before he left for work. He blamed himself for allowing the pressure at work to have taken its toll at home. He was also worried to find out how the children would react if word of their disagreement got to them. The thought of it really hurt him; he felt rotten inside. He felt his body temperature rise, and his head spun with dizziness. Jumping from his chair, he picked up his hat and walked out of the office straight to his car. He opened the door and got in.

"Where to, sir?" his chauffeur asked him.

"St. Francis clinic," he struggled to say. Immediately, without further questions, and noticing the countenance of his boss, the chauffeur started the ignition and drove straight to the clinic.

The ambassador was still pacing up and down his office, with a faxed document in his hand, looking as worried as ever. The events of the past few days had become more disturbing that he could hardly figure out what game Delano was playing with this band of inadequate and inexperienced militia. His intercom buzzed. He snapped it up.

"Hello?" he bellowed into the receiver. Delano's voice came on.

"Where the fucking hell have you been, you son…"

"Chief, were you able to get around?" Delano cut him off.

"Don't you play smart with me; I've been dead worried, and the home boys are on my fucking neck, and you don't feel you owe me an explanation?" he bellowed again.

"Chief, this ain't time for explanations. Note down the following. It's urgent."

"One minute," the ambassador scrambled for pen and paper. "Ok, go ahead," he ordered.

Delano gave him a description which he quickly penned down. At the clinic, the commissioner was placed on bed rest. He was attended to by his physician.

"Sir, you must really have tired yourself out. The test report before me shows a sharp fall in your blood pressure."

The commissioner's cell phone rang, interrupting him. The consulting doctor picked up the phone from the bedside desk and handed it to him. The commissioner clicked on the answering button and placed the phone to his ear.

"Hello?" a shaky voice spoke. "Meet me in church in two hours' time. Treat as urgent."

He recognised the priest's voice filtering into his ear.

"But…" the phone went dead before he could say more.

The doctor noticed his skin had turned pale.

"Sir, is there any problem?"

The commissioner hoisted himself from the little bed bearing his large frame.

"I got to go."

"But sir, you…"

"I will be fine, send the bill to me." He let himself out of the room hurriedly, walked out of the clinic and marched towards his car. He took his phone and made a call as he got into the car.

"Base," he just told the chauffeur.

The car stopped at the station. Everything seemed quiet and deserted. Only the light leading into the station was on. He looked at his wristwatch and noticed it was already late in the evening. Anxious, he asked the driver.

"What time is it, Joey?"

"Sir, it is five past seven and the day shift is gone. Thoughts ran through his head, so many thoughts and things to do, and one of those things was not to go to the church, as his assignment with the priest was over. He never liked him. Since the very day, the priest had been posted to the city and the central church, he always knew that there was something phony about him; right from the day he attended his first mass in the parish, but not to the extent of being a cultist. Instead of fighting for the rights of the masses and consoling them with the sermons of resurrection, he became one of the many evils that had impoverished them, all for the love of the black gold.

The same night he was directed to meet him was a sure moment that had set his mind away from religion. He often wondered what all those church and miracle sermons were all about, when even those who are supposed to chart a better cause and live an exemplary life are the very ones that had turned the trade into a money-making venture. He was on the verge of being swallowed up by his thoughts, when he heard the voice of his chauffeur distorting his reasoning.

"Sir, where are we headed?" was the simple question which brought him back from his wandering.

"STAAC," he said unconsciously.

"STAAC? where is that, sir?" the driver queried.

"Oh!" the commissioner exclaimed, not betraying any emotion. "St. Ambrose Assumption Church."

"That will be Airport road, sir," chipped in the chauffeur.

"Yes, Joey."

He reversed the car and drove out of the station.

The Range Rover SUV was parked at the entrance gate to the church. Its black colour acted as a camouflage that suited the night cover created by the night sky and the blackout from the National Power Holding Company (NPHC).

The occupants of the SUV sat agitated.

"Boss," one of the men with Delano called out to him. "I don't think this man will come, we better start going before we get busted by patrol officers." Delano looked at his watch. It was fifteen minutes past the two hours fixed for the commissioner's arrival.

"Five minutes, guys, I'm dead sure he will come. Five minutes, if he is not here, then we will zap, ok?" Delano said.

They nodded their heads. Some moments passed then a car drove into view and approached them. Another one showed up from behind with full head lights, confirming the arrival of the commissioner.

"Boys, get ready, here he is!" Delano alerted them. Immediately the man behind the wheel ignited the engine and returned the full light signal as confirmation to the car behind. The vehicle stationed itself in front of the church gate with full lights on, which blinded the commissioner's vision. All this was enough evidence to him, from his many years of police training both within and outside the country, that he had been deceived into a trap. He immediately took his smartphone out of his pocket and activated the GPS application device. He fumbled with the phone to get a number. At last he got hold of the number of the Brotherhood's Grand Patron and dialled it hurriedly. But the door of his car was flung open. Two of the militants jumped at him and ordered the chauffeur to move, and as they argued, the commissioner's phone fell to the floor.

The Grand Hotel was busy with various events on a daily basis. The event for the night was the official unveiling of a new addition to the Brotherhood. The Oasis Petrol and Gas Company, which had been registered and incorporated in Nigeria six months before, had been officially given a license for the importation of petroleum products into the country, under the aegis of the petroleum subsidy program; a program worth trillions of dollars. Yet the availability of the products and the incessant increase of pump prices, continued to give mixed feelings to numerous labour bodies in the country. The license issued to Oasis Petrol within six months of its establishment in the industry had generated questions from all quarters of the polity. Bigger companies had been on the queue for over four years, waiting for approval to get into the subsidy scheme, but nothing had happened for them. They were denied the license to operate under the subsidy program. High Chief Ugo Uzodinma, the Grand Patron of the

Brothers, hailed from one of the south eastern states of the country and was a major importer of hides and skin used for the manufacturing of goods. He was an importer of electronic products and an owner of many conglomerates both within and outside Nigeria.

He had enjoyed unwholesome romances with the multinational companies; one who had long fought for the rights of the Eastern presidency before it was given to a minority group, an act that had caused him to continue to fight everything that the government stood for. He vowed not to rest until the Igbo presidency project, which had long been a financer of the Brotherhood, was actualised in the country. When he decided to go into the oil and gas business, it became an easy task, as most of those who had benefitted from his windfall of money made it possible. As the official opening of the Oasis Group was under way, the high chief's phone rang. It was the commissioner. He walked away from the crowd of well-wishers who had come in numbers from all over the world to celebrate with him, went to a quiet place by the pool side, and answered the call. The line was activated, but no voice came from the other end. He cut the line.

"This is strange," he said to himself. He decided to call the military base commander. The drowsy voice of the commander showed that the man had been sleeping.

"Dotun is in trouble. Find him! Send the men now!" he ended the call and went over to attend to the day's business. He didn't want to be daunted by the current happenings. He walked back into the crowd. Someone who had been watching him walked up to him and whispered into his ear.

"What?" The high chief then patted him on the back. "The boys have been sent on their trail. Come, let's enjoy the night! Tomorrow we will deal with that." And they both walked back into the crowd. A wine girl approached them. Chief Ugo collected two glasses of wine from her tray and handed over one glass to his worried companion. He gulped the contents of his glass and placed it back on the tray, for he was a man who never allowed trivialities to disturb his moments of happiness, no matter what the consequences were. He always believed that money can make iron float, no matter how tough it was.

Disclosure

A group of armed men searched and ransacked the abandoned vehicle that lay at the concern of the Refinery Road Junction. Driving into the expressway through the roundabout, they turned into Uti Street, off 5th Junction road. A thorough search of the entire area, thanks to the GPS device they had picked up, was done with no result. The search proved abortive. No more clues leading to the abducted commissioner was found. The phone of an armed officer rang. He was going to take the call when he heard the GPS beep. He cut off the first call and activated the device. He ran a quick search, and found out that it was the commissioner's GPS that was connecting with his again. He immediately alerted the other officers on the search team.

"Guys, let's go! I've just picked up the signal of the phone again!" Immediately the band of officers jumped into the military van, and they drove off. Delano and his selected men took the blindfolded commissioner inside the warehouse, and placed him beside Father Chukwuma. Another woman with a blindfold on was wheeled into the warehouse and placed before the commissioner. Delano ordered the blindfolds of the two men to be removed. As this was done, the two men gasped for a breath of fresh air. Surprise almost took their breath away as they discovered one another.

"Father!"

It was the commissioner who shouted first. The priest looked away, feeling guilty for giving out information that had led to the capture of the commissioner by the groups of marauders. His exclamation drew the attention of the blindfolded woman who also shouted in a crying voice, "Dotun, is that you?" the woman asked.

Shocked and bewildered, the commissioner shouted in protest, "Please don't hurt my wife!" Delano ordered the blindfold to be removed from her face. When she got used to the light in the warehouse, she recognised her husband.

"Dotun, what are we doing here? Who are these men carrying guns everywhere?" she asked indignantly.

"Please, don't hurt her! She is all I have got. I will do anything you want me to."

Delano took the map from his pocket and showed it to the commissioner. "When is this hit going to take place?" he asked him.

The man looked at the map intently, and then tears silently rolled down his cheeks.

"Saturday, by midnight."

The soft sounds of footsteps peddled outside. Delano, who had been briefed about the ins and outs of the situation in the isolated warehouse, gave an inaudible command, and immediately two of the men took hold of the commissioner. They moved him out through the exit route that led to the riverside. As the last of them passed through the door, heavily-armed men from the Force burst into the warehouse. They immediately made swift moves to secure the whole place. The leader of the assault team shouted at the priest and the wife of the commissioner, "Where did they go?"

The priest pointed at the route that led through the back of the warehouse. The leader of the armed group ordered his men to go after them. After a quick check on the place to make sure it was safe, he picked up his phone and made a call to his superior.

"A priest and a woman were found, and they are safe in our custody. As for the commissioner, he's yet to be found. My men are on their trail." He listened to some more instructions from the other end of the phone. "Yes sir, I will sure do that; moving to base with the rescued victims; Awaiting to confirm the outcome of the mission from the other end, sir…ok sir, over and out." He looked at the men who surrounded him.

"Move them out!" he ordered.

"We return to base; waiting their arrival." They immediately untied the two prisoners and made a quick retreat from the warehouse. The road leading to the river bank of the isolated village was difficult to use because of overgrown grasses and a soft muddy ground, wet from the rain that had grossly showered during their stay at the warehouse. The light from the torch Delano and his men carried suddenly became dim. As they travelled through the bush path, they heard footsteps running towards them.

They tried hard to bear the uncooperative commissioner along. The band of men suddenly stopped; they had to make a quick decision on what to do. The sound from the ruffled bushes leading towards them kept getting louder and louder and the voices of their pursuers became clearer. The militants with Delano finally decided that he should bear the commissioner and head towards the boat waiting by the river bank. Delano took the commissioner from the guys.

They heard the sound of sporadic gunshots, killing two of the militants. Immediately the others took cover and exchanged bullets with the approaching armed military officers. Delano headed towards the boat. The gun battle which ensued left four other militants dead, and left a lot of casualties among the attacking armed force men too. Delano carried the commissioner all through rough terrain leading right to the bank of the river. His steps became slow, as blood stains covered him. He managed to approach the boat, but collapsed under the weight of the heavy man. The pilot of the boat rushed to him.

The commissioner struggled to get on to his feet, but the rope tied around his ankles made it difficult for him; the soil which was wet and slippery also made it difficult for him to gain balance, and he kept tripling over. The pilot rushed to help the incapacitated Delano and tugged him into the boat. After a short while, he came back for the commissioner, who had managed to get on his feet and was hopping back through the dark path that had taken them to the river bank. He had but one goal to be run into by the chasing troops of the armed officers. But he was caught and dragged back into the boat, and they sped off, away into the dark, calm night.

Closing In

The morning that followed was a special one at the office. The news of the commissioner's kidnapping had spread like wildfire, consuming everything in its wake. The team of investigating Police from the Central Investigating Bureau (C.I.B) swarmed everywhere in the office to try and get clues that might give insight into the kidnapping of the serving police commissioner, one whom the entire Force regarded as one of the best. The information given to the Police by his rescued wife and the priest did not reveal much about the event. The priest was released by one of the rescuing team officers, an infiltrated member of the Brotherhood who left him with a strong warning not to say anything. As for the wife of the abducted commissioner, the bad state of her health made it very difficult for her to remember the night the kidnappers visited their home; rounded up the security personnel and her cook; and took her hostage.

Joey the driver could only remember that he had driven the man down to St. Ambrose's Assumption Church and had observed a vehicle shining its lights brightly on their path. When he made a move to open the door that night, he was greeted by a heavy thud from a gun butt.

Father Chukwuma was more of an idiot, as the investigating officers could not deduce anything meaningful from the cocktail of lies that he served them; a tale of how he heard shouts from people outside the gates of the Church and had rushed to the scene, seeking to get an audience with heavily armed men. Those "soldiers" were harassing his church members, who were going home after mass. He was ordered to enter the vehicle of the kidnappers, and they whisked him off to an unknown location. All evidence gotten from these men didn't help to prove anything of any sort, making it difficult for the Police to do their job. Twelve hours had elapsed now, and the investigating team was becoming worried because of the nature and ways of the kidnappers. Unlike the other cases of kidnapping, where the kidnappers contacted the family of the victim, stating their ransom, they had claimed nothing. The police officers had waited, and yet they had received no calls and no e-mails.

Everyone was anxious. No one knew if he was still alive. The team sent to sweep the area in the early hours of the morning returned with news of bloodstains all over the surrounding bushes. They also found a pair of shoes on the river bank. Como and some of the generals from other, smaller camps all over the creek, who had been informed of the failure of the Bongola project, assembled in his office.

They finished finalising plans on a counter attack to defend the Bongola port. The attack was to take place in less than eighteen hours. They argued over the need for them to move in and surprise the Brotherhood who had planned to make an attack on the Bongola field by cutting off the access route to that field. Como's insistence that Delano must reappear before they closed up on the attack caused heated arguments, as other members of the Bongola port operation perceived waiting for Delano as a delay tactic; a wrong tactic which might compromise the protection of the Bongola port. The argument became so intense that Como threatened the pact and the oneness of the group, and stormed out of the conference hall.

Delano lay on the bed in his room; his left hand in heavy bandage. Jade was sitting beside him on the bed, watching him as he slept innocently; unaware of the trouble in the creeks that was threatening the very fabric of Como's unit. He trembled slightly. This startled Jade, who gazed at him, wondering at his state. Delano suddenly woke up and screamed, scrambling for the nearest exit. Jade tried everything in her power to hold him down.

"It's ok, it's ok!" she said.

"No, no, you are dead!" Delano kept shouting.

Como suddenly opened the door and walked in to see both of them struggling. He rushed over to them and helped keep Delano down, so as not to aggravate his injured arm.

"It is ok, Delano. It is her," Como announced quietly.

"No! I saw her dead. I carried her myself!" Delano shouted.

"I know that," Como continued. "I will explain everything to you. Just relax, ok, and you will get to know everything, ok, but for now relax, so you won't aggravate your wound." Delano became calm and continued to gaze at Jade, his eyes roving from one person to the other.

He asked Como, "What about the commissioner?" Como looked at him but didn't answer his question.

"Jade will bring you some food, and when you have finished eating, we will be waiting for you in the conference room.

"Jade?" Delano murmured, looking at her. Como nodded and stood up.

"I will leave you two alone now," he said and walked out of the room.

The door of the conference room flung open. Delano walked in in the company of Jade, his arm still in a sling. His mind still reeled from the pain of his wound. Surprised, he discovered the faces of people he never seen before. He slowly moved to a vacant chair and Jade drew it out for him. She went round the room and took another vacant chair directly opposite him.

"I guess both of you understand yourselves now and you now know some of the mysteries that escaped you," Como started.

"So you, people, had all this planned out! And you conspired to pull a prank on me from the onset! And you got me involved in your god-forsaken battle!" Delano exclaimed. They smiled.

"So the dead girl, that night, who was she?" he asked.

"Let's leave that for now," Como hushed. These men you see seated here are drafted from all the units within the riverine area for the Bongola attack operation which is taking place tonight."

"Tonight?" exclaimed Delano. Como ignored him.

"We were waiting for your recovery to get your input on the plan. So now you are here, what do you think?" Como asked him, as the others turned their attention towards him.

"We will go ahead with the haggle." He stood up from his chair, still tired, yet his vision clear. He groaned under the pain from his wounded hand.

"I need to send a message across to the Embassy. Will you excuse me?" He walked away. The others looked at one another in surprise.

The country home of High Chief Uzo was a beehive of early callers from the Brotherhood of Barons. Most of them, who had heard about the case of the kidnapped commissioner, knowing the sensitive position of the man to the survival of their various endeavours, wanted reassurance concerning the safety of the huge investments they had contributed to the affair. They also wanted to know what it meant for them, if the commissioner was forced to give away information that would eventually reveal their secrets. The other groups of callers, not so much involved in investments but supporting the course because of their political ambition for the next general election, were also present. They were those who did their best to discredit the current president on the basis that he had not lived up to his electoral promises. They were also there to know when the proposed attack on the Bongola port would be carried out, for they knew that the success of the attack would not only cast a big shadow on the inability of the government to protect lives and property, but also give them the political onus they needed to hinge their electoral campaign on.

They sat there with gloomy faces, unable to take their drinks. The only thing on their minds was answers. They needed answers, and they wanted them now. The high chief walked into the living room, all smiles, and welcomed them.

"Brothers," he greeted them. But he was met with a cold reception. He knew at once that this wasn't the time for fooling around. Immediately he skipped the formalities and went straight to address them.

"In all our years of operations, there has never been a time like this; a time when our collective resolve has been so tested, especially now that we are on the verge of a new beginning, and we see our fortunes changing for the best. Let me assure you that this is nothing compared to what we have gone through before, not just with this event of the kidnapping of our most trusted secret agent, but with the probe and counter probe by the members of the House. Information reaching us shows that Commissioner Adedotun is still alive and has not divulged any information to his captors. For now, we don't really know if it is the white man who is connected with his disappearance or the militants, but one thing I can tell you for sure, is that he has kept our little secret. Let me assure you, in the absence of the commissioner, the Brotherhood has requested the express services of Kiddo to handle the forthcoming haggle, while the services of the Special Anti-Military Force are to move in on the Bongola mission. Be reminded that all logistics have been put in place…"

"Chief…," Alhaji Usman Megeri interrupted. Megeri was one of the power brokers from the northern part of the country, whose contribution and membership in the Brotherhood extended beyond the oil and gas business. His political ambition was overwhelming, as he dreamt of becoming the next president of the Republic. All the members knew his passion for power, because he once served as a military ruler. The man had vowed as a matter of personal interest that he would rule as a civilian head, in order to help balance the scales with the Southwest. What did that mean exactly? Anytime he was asked, he was unable to give a satisfactory explanation.

Another reason why he was so revered among the Brotherhood was that he had an agenda threatening the existence of the Brotherhood even more than that of the militants, through his links with Al-Qaeda and the Islamic State, the dreaded Islamic group of terrorists whose activities have endangered the very foundation of peace all over the world. The Brotherhood knew that men were already being trained to carry out terrorist activities. In the wake of his inability to become president, he could, through this group, make the country ungovernable. The explanations just given by the high chief had not gone down well with Megeri, so he had to make a remark, as he always did in such gatherings. A characteristic some of his colleagues admired in him was that, whenever there was such a gathering, they could depend on him to always speak their minds.

When he cut off the high chief, the others all sat up, knowing that the Alhaji was ready to rain down fire.

"You said the commissioner has not divulged any information. How do you know this? Anything we have to do we must be sure of, because a lot is at stake here, and no one, and I mean no one, would want to be fooled by stories. None of us would want to go to jail either after all we have done for the Brotherhood."

The murmurs from the others showed their views tallied with what the Alhaji had just said. Sensing that he had the support of his colleagues, as usual, he continued.

"So chief, tell us the truth. Has the commissioner actually not divulged any information that may incriminate any of us here, which also includes you, or are you just trying to make all this look nice and keep us all calm, thank you?" He gathered his Agbada around himself with an air of self-satisfaction, even though the way he spoke English, was corrupted by the interference of his mother tongue. He launched back into his seat. Chief Uzo stood up for the second time to address the issue of the secrecy of the Brotherhood which the commissioner was privy to. An issue that was now the centre of the debate, as agreed to by the members from the question raised by Alhaji Megeri.

He was clearing his throat to start answering them, when suddenly his cell phone rang. He checked who was calling, but saw an unknown number. He looked at his Brothers, who looked at him questioningly. "It is an unknown number," he said rhetorically. He hesitated for a while and answered the call. The voice of Como assaulted his ear, "We have the commissioner."

Chief Uzo immediately hit on the speaker button so all in the room could hear the conversation.

"Did you hear what I've just said?" Como's voice thundered through the speaker.

"Who are you and where are you? And what do you want?" Chief Uzo rolled out the questions everyone expected to be answered.

"Shut up and listen, and of course listen good you blood-sucker and killer of innocent women and children," Como ordered.

"This is what you are to do. Tonight, you will go to the leisure park with the U.S. Ambassador, and there we shall haggle for our goods. Don't bother to call the Police, because if you do, then your secret will not only get to the presidency, but we will also bury you all. Bring the U.S. Ambassador, and your secret will remain buried with us forever."

"Tonight…," Chief Uzo stuttered, "What time exactly?"

"You will wait for further instructions."

"But at least, can I get to know your nam…"

The phone abruptly went dead, rudely cutting the high chief off.

The National Security Adviser, General Musa Kanemi, Rtd., sat in his office, attending to some of the day's papers his secretary had just brought in. The news of the commissioner's kidnapping had become mince-meat for the national dailies. The most captivating title was in the cover story by the *Niger-Delta Focus,* a soft sell newspaper of the region. The eye witness account had given a vivid detail of how the commissioner had supposedly been kidnapped, as if the witness had been present at the time of the kidnapping.

While reading the paper, the general wondered about the masterful way the reporter had culled the story. His mind pondered on what must have necessitated the kidnapping of the commissioner. His intercom buzzed. He heard the voice of his secretary.

"The Director General is here, sir," she said.

"Let him in," the NSA replied, and he tidied up his table to welcome the visitor.

The door opened revealing the Director General of the anti-graft body who walked into the office.

"Good day, sir," he greeted, as he walked up to the adviser, hand stretched out for a handshake.

"Good day, D.G," he replied, as he shook his hand warmly.

"Please, do take your seat," he said offering him the couch in the spacious room. He threw the "Niger-Delta Focus" on his lap.

"I guess you are not new to that story?" the D.G looked at the headline.

"I have read it, but why are these boys behaving like this?" he queried.

"This morning the Presidency received a distress call from the boys in the creeks, and a mail sent from the US Embassy. In that mail was a list of Nigerians who, they claimed, have aided and abetted the multinational companies in the exploration and exploitation of the resources, and the marginalisation of both the government and the people of the region. The Presidency wants you and your men to go and arrest all those who have, in one way or another, been fingered on the list here…" He drew out a list from his suit and handed it over to the D.G. The D.G went through the list intently, and sighed heavily.

"But sir, I thought the Joint Force was responsible for these actions?" he interjected.

"The report reaching us shows that our Force has been seriously compromised by these forces of powerful, wealthy men who are bent on sabotaging the efforts of the government on the present issue of amnesty. For it seems they are against the granting of amnesty to these present monsters called militancy, so D.G, you have the express permission and support of the highest office in the land to move in on these people and bring them in before the end of the day."

The D.G looked on with great interest as he addressed him.

"All the logistics that you may need are being processed, and in the next few minutes, they will be made available to you." The over sixty, bald man, with grey hair daunting the few patches of the remaining hair on his head, stood up and walked towards his work station.

"Director that will be all; please remember that the Presidency trusts you and believes in you on this matter. I hope you won't let him down. He won't take failure for an answer."

"Not at all, sir, I and my men are swinging into action immediately," the D.G replied.

"Good, that will be all, then," the NSA concluded.

The D.G got up, walked up to him, shook hands and then left the office. The NSA, making sure he had gone far enough, picked up his cell phone and made a call.

"Cover has been seriously compromised, and the Presidency has promised to bring down all those who have jeopardised the very existence of the Federation. I advise that everyone should go underground as soon as possible, as I plan to do so myself. I will meet you in the next fifteen minutes at the Spot place." He listened and replied, "Yes, I was able to expunge your name and a few others from the list, so they won't be coming for you."

He listened again.

"Ok, I will be with you in fifteen minutes." He ended the call and plunged into his chair, then blew hot air to the sky.

The late evening was one that had a lot to reveal about the events of the day. The tense atmosphere devoid of the streaming winds and the chirping sounds of birds heralded the events of the night. The commanding officer of the naval base had just concluded the inspection of his troops for the secure Bongola port operation from details handed to him from the naval headquarters as a result of the prompting from the Presidency, who had received a detailed fax from the American Embassy on the attack. Discreetly, he divided his men into two groups. The first was to meet Delano and Como on the site of the exchange of prisoners and hostages held by the militants, as well as the kidnapped commissioner and the U.S. Ambassador. The other set of officers were to close up with the militias already stationed on the mouth of the Niger, awaiting their arrival. Delano and his men under the command of Como made their way to their vessel en-route the oil facility on the high sea. Dressed up in full regalia, they all carried AK47, Beretta CX4 rifles, except for Spoonface, Banga and Shaka who carried RPG-7 (rocket propelled grenade) guns and rolls of ammunitions across their shoulders, and Delano, who managed to carry a Colt 45 Rampant pistol despite his injured hand. They had pieces of palm leaves set across their lips, when they filed out in a straight line towards the Crocodile which had been prepared for the night mission.

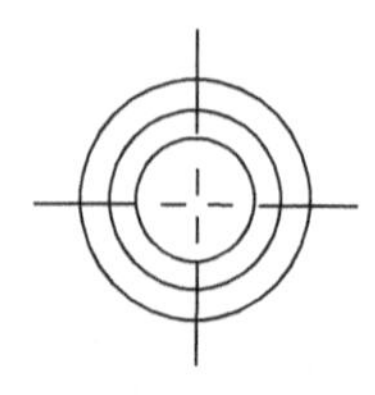

Nemesis

Delano and the host of militants filed up inside the partially lit, abandoned fishery house. They sat down on the log of decayed wood that characterised the interior of the house. With them were the masked commissioner and the hostages during the raid of the MV Princess. They were heavily armed with AK 47, Beretta CX4 assort rifles and guns. The fierce, hungry, deprived-looking men all awaited the arrival of the Commander of the Joint Federal Force, who incidentally was the requested mercenary Sergeant Malaya Rogers (aka Kiddo), who had abducted the U.S. Ambassador with the support of the late Davis; an action which had degenerated into the event which had finally led him to finish the unfinished business he started.

Delano looked at his wristwatch as it ticked away. He cast a subtle glance at Como, who returned it agitated. The big double door leading to the warehouse suddenly opened and two police officers filed in. They carried a pair of outdated rifles which had apparently been out of use since the colonial masters had left the shores of the country. Kiddo also walked inside with the police officer hurriedly appointed to the task by the Brotherhood. One of the men, who carried a huge bag, went to the front of the line and dropped it on the floor with a heavy thud. A voice yelled out of the bag. Delano rushed towards the bag.

"Not so fast, my friend," Kiddo shouted. Two of his men drew out their weapons. Delano came to a halt and walked back into the file.

"First, let's see the hostages!" Kiddo said, grinning.

Delano and Como exchanged glances. Como then nodded to one of the boys standing behind the file of hostages, whose faces were covered with masks. Four of the hostages' masks were pulled off, revealing the commissioner, the captain and three of his men taken from the MV Princess.

Convinced, Kiddo ordered his man to open the bag. The police sergeant dragged the bag and opened it. The pale-looking U.S. Ambassador, hands tied behind his back, gasped for breath. Kiddo ordered his men to go over and release the hostages.

"Let them loose and bring them over here!" Kiddo shouted to his men, who moved swiftly towards the hostages.

"I know you will honour your part of the bargain. You, Americans, always do. That is one silly thing about you, people; always honest to a fault," the robust Kiddo, commented with a broad smile. He giggled, turned and looked at the remaining officers who sandwiched him.

"Put him back into the bag, and bring him along!"

As they rushed and forced the U.S. Ambassador back into the bag, the rest of the militants, disguised with face masks like the hostages, pulled off their masks and took hold of the policemen sent to release the commissioner. They grabbed their guns. Delano, Como and the rest of the boys brought out their guns and ordered them to lie down.

"Get him out of the bag," Como ordered two of his men, who immediately rushed, ripped the bag open and helped the U.S. Ambassador out, untying him.

"We are not, after all, as stupid as you, people, who think with their minds and not their hearts," Delano said, as he walked towards the transfixed Kiddo. He stopped and gazed at the U.S. Ambassador.

"You ok?" he asked. The pale, fragile man nodded to him.

"I bet you won't be so lucky," he added, punching Kiddo in the belly. "That is for distrust." He punched him a second time. Kiddo grunted in pain. "That is for Davis." And a final punch sent Kiddo crashing to the floor. He grunted in pain again. "That is for the innocent women and children that your activities have made homeless and hopeless." He walked back to the U.S. Ambassador.

A few kilometres away from the location of the haggle, the men of the Naval Force dispatched by the commander were on their way with heavily armed men. Surprisingly, Kiddo stood up in a brisk movement. He pounced on Delano, knocked him to the floor, and started punching him.

Some of the other militants rushed to help him. Como ordered to leave them alone. Delano tried hard to get rid of Kiddo. Standing up with his nose bleeding, he took the sling off his injured hand. Clinching his fist, he beckoned to Kiddo to advance towards him. As Kiddo rushed to him again, Delano struck him on the face. Kiddo staggered back. The men stood, watching them engage in fist fight, sensing that Delano would overpower him. Kiddo made a move for a gun held by one of his men, but before he could wrestle the gun from the officer, Como shot his left thigh. Kiddo fell on the floor, screaming, and Como ordered his men to seize him. At that precise moment, the door of the warehouse burst open, and men from the naval base rushed in, encircling them.

"Put you guns down!" one of the officers shouted out to them. Como and his boys hesitated. Como turned to Delano and shouted, "You've betrayed us!"

Delano looked at him intently. Their eyes locked. The officer in charge of the batch of military men walked through from behind. He went straight to Delano.

"Operation Secure Bongola (OSB) is safe now. We have orders to bring you and your men to base," he requested of him.

"The President is ready to meet you and debrief you on the demand you sent to him through the American Embassy." This elicited a loud shout and jubilation from the rest of the boys. Como watched Delano shake hands with him.

"Thank you," Como, stunned, could only say.

"Our crew is waiting. Shall we?" the leading rescuing officer asked. "Boys, take him and the commissioner as well, and these hostages".

He led the way out of the warehouse, and the others followed him.

High Chief Uzo sat in his oval office made of fine oakwood and tastefully decorated. He was in a pensive mood, as he had not heard anything from either the attack on the Bongola facility or the exchange of the hostages kidnapped by the militants. He especially had heard no news yet of the commissioner. The rate of phone calls from business partners, stakeholders and members of the Brotherhood all over the world, although it distracted him, had not helped. Some called to reiterate their support. The overly selfish ones among them had been calling to rain down thunder and brimstone in the eventuality that their investments should go down the drain. He wished he could just switch off his phones, but that wasn't possible. His next move and action solely depended on the call he was waiting for. The phone rang at last. He picked it up, as he always did since the initiation of the operations, hoping to hear good news of the operations. But once again there was no good news.

"Hello, Alhaji Mergeri…"

The Alhaji, in his characteristic manner, ignored him and shouted from the other end, "Chief, all our members have been arrested by the government anti-crime agency, and I think they are closing in on us."

"What?! Arrested? Where are you now?"

"Chief, I'm on my way out of the country. I will call you once I get to my new destination, which I don't know right now." And the phone went dead.

"Hello, hello?" Chief Uzo shouted into the mouthpiece. There was no reply, only the humming sound of a phone that was still engaged. He wondered what must have happened at the other end. The sudden way the phone at the other end had gone dead kept puzzling the high chief, who paced up and down his office. It was close to midday, and yet no report on any of the operations.

"Who has ordered the arrest and why have they been arrested?" he asked himself again and again. He was still buried in thought when his phone rang yet again.

The programmed tune indicated that it was the National Security Adviser that was calling. He rushed to the phone on his work station.

"Hello?" he answered.

"Wherever you are, start leaving the country…," was all he could hear before the line went dead.

"What the hell is going on?" he shouted rhetorically. He tried to reach the National Security Adviser again. Just then, there was a knock on the door. He froze and waited.

The knock came again, and the only thing the chief could think of was to escape. He walked to the pile of books on his bookshelf. Pulling out one of the large books on the shelf, he pressed a button inside, and it split open, revealing an exit. The chief hurriedly gathered his belongings, picked up his briefcase, and zapped through the door. The men of the agency on the other side of the door waited but got no response. Then they decided to do the only logical thing. They broke the door and rushed in to discover an empty room. Looking everywhere for possible evidence, they found nothing.

The military jet that brought all the parties from the delta to the seat of government touched down on the private landing space within the Villa. Como and Delano, in the company of the freed U.S. Ambassador, and the serving American Ambassador to Nigeria, who came with the Naval Chief, were ushered into a waiting Nissan SUV, and driven to the State House. The President and his Ministers had been waiting for them since the Naval Chief had called to inform them that they were on their way, to welcome them in a press conference. Delano, sandwiched by Como, presented the document. The President received the paper with overwhelming enthusiasm. The assistance of the American had enabled them to unmask those behind the kidnapping of the American U.S. Ambassador and the big oil cartel. The President promised the full corollaries of the law would follow their course on all those who had been indicted in the report from the Niger Delta, and there would be no sacred cow. A panel of enquiries was immediately set up by the President to look into the activities of the multinationals as well as all their allies, and to come up with a blueprint for the development of the oil rich region of the country. He bestowed on Delano the highest military decoration of the Federal Republic of Nigeria.

The End

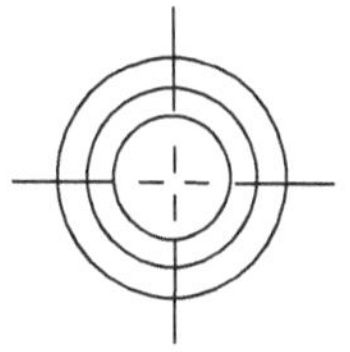

Acknowledgements

I want to expressly, with all humility, thank the Creator Jehovah for the gift He has given me and His help in seeing that this work comes to fruition. In the course of writing this book, I have met too many people to name them all. The length of this work will not allow me to thank all of them. However, there are people who have contributed in large and small ways, directly and indirectly to the success of this work; these I cannot forget in a hurry. First on this list of indebtedness is Dr. Charles Edogue, for reading and re-reading this manuscript to ascertain that the flow of thought was coherent; then my indefatigable, Brigitte Poirson, and Idolor Omo Henry who were my companions during the closing stage of writing this book, and who sat straight from late night into the early hours of the morning, sharing ideas on the work.

My thanks go to Captain E.S Ogbebor (Rtd.); I appreciate the concern and immense assistance offered in the cohesion of the story. I will not forget the loving chatter with my family members and my friends, Sandra Afoghen, Chinedu Ogwu, Ekukinam Joseph, Okotie Henry, Hon. Justice Irikefe Iyasere, Bethel Zidougha and Tesi Arubi, PhD. Osopkor Tony, you are not left out. I also appreciate the amazing team at Winepress, an imprint of Noirledge Publishing who turned this roughneck into a jewel. If there is anyone not mentioned, know that it wasn't a deliberate act, but sheer oversight didn't allow me to remember you all. However, if there is one thing you must know, it should be that my love and heartfelt appreciation goes out to you all.

Akpoviri Akpoveta Prince, commonly known by his pen name, Don Veta, is an award-winning Nigerian writer, playwright, filmmaker and multimedia consultant who is using his work to address the many ills in the society. A *Cobbler's Travails*, his first published literary work was 1st Runner-up for the 2020 Association of Nigerian Authors Prize for Drama.

An eclectic writer whose works cut through creative literary genres, Don Veta is a recipient of an Excellence Award by the Nigerian Top Executives in the Entertainment and Media Industry for his contributions to the creative industry. *Guerrilla of the Niger Delta*, an action-filled historical thriller, is his most recent literary work.

www.ingramcontent.com/pod-product-compliance
Lightning Source LLC
Chambersburg PA
CBHW070519160726
48003CB00004B/1633